CHIMERA CLASH

CHIMERA CLASH

THE ORIGIN STORY OF MONSTERS™ BOOK THREE

MARTHA CARR
MICHAEL ANDERLE

This book is a work of fiction. All of the characters, organizations, and events portrayed in this novel are either products of the author's imagination or are used fictitiously. Sometimes both.

Copyright © 2023 LMBPN Publishing
Cover Art by Jake @ J Caleb Design
http://jcalebdesign.com / jcalebdesign@gmail.com
Cover copyright © LMBPN Publishing
A Michael Anderle Production

LMBPN Publishing supports the right to free expression and the value of copyright. The purpose of copyright is to encourage writers and artists to produce the creative works that enrich our culture.

The distribution of this book without permission is a theft of the author's intellectual property. If you would like permission to use material from the book (other than for review purposes), please contact support@lmbpn.com. Thank you for your support of the author's rights.

LMBPN Publishing
PMB 196, 2540 South Maryland Pkwy
Las Vegas, NV 89109

Version 1.00, March 2023
ebook ISBN: 979-8-88541-162-2
Print ISBN: 979-8-88878-269-9

DON'T MISS OUR NEW RELEASES

Join the LMBPN email list to be notified of new releases and special promotions (which happen often) by following this link:

http://lmbpn.com/email/

THE CHIMERA CLASH TEAM

Thanks to our JIT Readers

Dave Hicks
Dorothy Lloyd
Jackey Hankard-Brodie
Jan Hunnicutt

Editor

SkyFyre Editing Team

CHAPTER ONE

This wasn't Halsey Ambrosius' first time in a Turkish bazaar. It *was* her first time navigating the narrow walkways of a marketplace like this while carrying so many secrets in her pocket. Figuratively *and* literally.

The Grand Bazaar in Istanbul was Turkey's largest and most bustling marketplace, packed with vendors hawking their wares. Sparkling jewelry, colorfully dyed clothing, perfumes, rugs, household silver, bespoke hats and shoes, statues, carvings, knickknacks, and antiques. The pungent scent of Mediterranean spices choked the air, flavoring Halsey's every breath until she forgot she'd ever smelled anything else. Beneath it all was a strong undercurrent of roasted lamb, way too much lemon, and the acrid, sweaty stink of hundreds of people crowded so close together in a place that sold everything under the sun.

The hot and semi-dry Turkish sun.

Nothing a little personal elemental cooling system can't fix.

Walking closely beside her through the shouting, clanging, whistling, thumping of stacked crates, and hiss of fatty meats skewered and hung over a hot grill, Halsey's cousin Brigham wrinkled his nose as an enormous, shirtless man barreled through a narrow walkway between tents and covered stalls. "Yeesh. You see that guy?"

"Kinda hard not to," she muttered.

"First of all…" He ticked off points on his fingers, turning back once to catch a final glimpse of the man in question. "It's hot as balls out here. You don't see *me* walking around like that, parading a pair of glistening pecs before shoving people outta the way."

Halsey smirked as she scanned a table covered in fine Turkish jewelry. "What pecs?"

"Second—*hey*…" Brigham's dubious frown *almost* looked convincing until he gave up and snorted. "I have pecs."

"Feel free to keep 'em to yourself."

"No shit. Should've told *him* that."

She shook her head with a polite smile at the woman behind the jewelry stand before she and her cousin moved on.

"Way to deflect, by the way," Brigham murmured, then laughed when she elbowed him in the ribs. "I'm not done."

"Of course not."

"*Second*," he continued as he shot her a pert look. "It's plain unsanitary."

Halsey snorted and stepped out of the way as an elderly man pushing a brilliantly painted cart of fresh baklava rolled past. Two of the cart's old wheels squeaked intermittently along the uneven cobblestones. "Let me get this straight. You see an insanely built Turk walking through a bazaar with his shirt off, and your biggest issue with it is *cleanliness*? Have you seen this place?"

"Well, yeah." He looked down and happened to come upon an empty, discarded box of some type of cracker, which he kicked to send the cardboard skittering across the stones. "Still, it's not like...the streets of *Mexico* or anything."

"Dude." Halsey frowned playfully, then looked past him at a mostly enclosed storefront selling genuine Turkish rugs. "If you're gonna start making gross comparisons like that—"

"Yes. Gross. That's what I'm *saying.*"

"—then at least pick an actual city or a specific region. Otherwise, it's lazy."

"Wait, wait, wait. Hold on." Brigham pointed at her as they passed the rug shop and hardly spared it a second glance. "You think wanting a certain standard of hygiene is *lazy?*"

"I think stereotyping an entire country based on *one* crazy night in Tepito is beneath you."

"Fine. I'm just sayin'. We've been walking across the city for the last hour, and I'm already soaked enough to drink my own shirt. Look." He spread his arms and looked pointedly at his loose linen garment, which was more damp with sweat than dry. "The last thing I need is some other dude and his *glistening pecs* dripping all over me because he didn't feel like wearing the same layers as everyone else. Seriously, Hal. There are *kids* here. And *food*. You want somebody like him standing over the grill while you're waiting for Muhammed to get the perfect crisp on your shish kebab?"

"I think this conversation is over."

Her cousin laughed. "Fine. You're right. Wouldn't see *that* in Mexico."

"Probably because you won't find shish kebabs in Mexico. Not like here."

A dreamy, hazy smile passed across Brigham's face as he gazed toward the end of the walkway. "Man, gotta love Mexico City, though. Chupacabra or no, that was one hell of a night."

"Yet obviously not dirty enough to keep you from—watch it!"

Two young men around the cousins' age in their early twenties barreled down the narrow walkway on the back of a moped. Halsey grabbed Brigham's arm and yanked him to the side just in time to avoid becoming double-roadkill in a back alley of a Turkish bazaar. Their backs thumped against the solid wall behind them, the first they'd seen since making it past the marketplace's outer ring of vendors. The moped raced past them, ruffling the cousins' hair and sending a spray of dirt and small pebbles against their shins.

Only when the two young men had passed them did the driver lay on the vehicle's high-pitched, unimposing horn. The warbling *beep* echoed down the alley alongside the buzzing whine of the moped's engine.

Brigham shoved away from the wall and shouted after them, "The horn comes *before* you pass somebody, genius. It means, 'Coming through,' not, '*Sorry!*'" He spun toward Halsey and tossed his hands in exasperation. "How hard is that to understand?"

"I don't know…" She straightened and peered down the

alley to see another small cluster of pedestrians jump out of the way to avoid being run down. *Then* the driver beeped two more times. By then, he and his carefree passenger had disappeared into the throng of shoppers, vendors, and hagglers. "Say it in Turkish next time, and they might consider it. Maybe."

Brigham scowled down the walkway in the direction they'd been heading. Then he closed his eyes, inhaled deeply, and released a long, slow exhale. "Happy thoughts."

Halsey fought a laugh. "What?"

When her cousin opened his eyes again, all traces of his irritation had vanished. His eyes were wide and bright again as he flashed her one of his signature grins and gestured toward all the tents and stalls and tables ahead of them. "After you, cuz."

She scrutinized him and slowly walked past him to continue their journey deep into the center of the massive marketplace. "What happy thoughts?"

"Mine."

"Oh, come on…"

"Nope. No way." Brigham shook his head as they fell into step among the streams of pedestrians and the occasional vehicle squeezing through the densely packed stalls and tents. "They're called happy thoughts for a reason, Hal. Multiple reasons, if I'm honest, and one of them is the fact that I'm the only one with a few *very specific* happy thoughts in my head. So forget it."

"Yeah, okay…" Halsey's reply was an automatic response because now *she* had gotten distracted.

Brigham noticed and snorted as they passed a small but incredibly loud group of middle-aged women speaking in dizzyingly fast Turkish as they pointed at stacked cages of individual hens. "Okay, yeah. I get it. Keep our eye on the prize, right?"

"Uh...yeah." It wasn't usually this hard for her to stay engaged in a conversation. Brigham was her partner in Ambrosius militia monster-hunting missions, who also happened to be her best friend. Most of the time, they were on the same page and enjoyed a similar sense of humor.

Most of the time, they didn't hide things from each other.

Today was different, at least for Halsey. That made being distracted by an additional secret, *personal* mission easier. Especially now that she'd caught a glimpse of what she'd been looking for without her cousin knowing about it.

Far ahead, beyond dozens of erected tents, colorful flags, and flashy signs vying to grab potential new customers' attention, silver flashed in the sunlight when a light, warm breeze fluttered a few tent walls aside.

The Iyi Çay. *Silver sign. Past the hookah shop. Then ask for Aydem.*

Sure enough, the hookah shop in question was coming up on their right. Several customers were seated at small café tables or on piles of cushions, making use of the flavorful smoking devices.

Okay, so the tea tent isn't far ahead.

While Halsey silently calculated how much farther, hoping the flash of silver she'd seen actually belonged to the sign she was looking for, her cousin kept talking.

"Yeah, yeah. Good idea, cuz. Focus. We got a lotta people to impress back home, right?" He scoffed at his own joke and shook his head. "Right. Not like you're ever trying to impress anyone anyway."

"True," she replied as she scanned the narrowing alley ahead. Years of experience as Brigham's partner had taught her when to insert any response at all to keep her cousin engaged enough not to notice her tuning him out. At least when he was on gabby rants like this one.

"Anyway, you know what I mean. First official mission in almost three months now, right? The Ambrosius Clan finally opened their doors again," Brigham shouted, spreading his arms as if this was the announcement all the pedestrians in Istanbul had shown up to hear. "And they sent their A-Team to handle the first—"

A pillowing cloud of thick, white hookah vapor distracted him as they passed the shop. The sweet, fruity, cloying scent made him pause, and he sniffed the air before eyeing the recreational smoking devices that looked like lamps topped with burning coals instead of a lampshade. "Wow. What *is* that? Hey, Hal. You ever try one of these before? Hal?"

When he realized his cousin had continued through the bazaar without him, he jumped and scanned the faces of the closest pedestrians. He quickly recognized her long, dark, wavy hair and the olive-green canvas jacket he couldn't believe she'd worn in this heat. He leapt after her with a laugh. "Hey!"

Halsey was barely aware of her cousin's shout, but she slowed anyway and pretended to be interested in the stacks of old paperback books that seemed out of place in a marketplace like this. They were all written in Turkish, so she couldn't focus on the titles. That didn't matter to the shriveled elderly man with sagging skin who watched her from behind the stacks of books.

"What are you doing?" Brigham asked as he caught up to her. "You don't read Turkish."

"That doesn't mean I can't still look." She smiled at the man behind the books before they kept walking like they were looking for something a little more specific. Of course, they *were*, and there was one further secret item on Halsey's list. No one knew about it except the person she was supposed to meet today inside Iyi Çay. Alone.

Since the minute they'd entered the bazaar, it had proven more difficult than she'd expected to casually and naturally ditch her cousin in the chaos of the busy marketplace.

Get him talking, Hal. Once he's on a roll, it should be easy. As long as there aren't any more distractions between here and there.

That seemed unlikely in a place as bustling, loud, and hectic as this. Still, she had an appointment to keep, so she had to try.

She nudged her cousin's arm and shot him a crooked smile. "You were saying?"

"Yeah, I was." Brigham chuckled and wiped the sweat from his forehead with the back of a hand. "What was I saying?"

"Ambrosius Clan opening their doors, and out comes the A-Team."

"Right." He pointed at her and winked. "Which is us, by the way."

"Oh, good. I was starting to wonder…"

"Very funny." His gaze settled on another pop-up food

stand, this one selling *kofta* meatballs, and he shook his head. "Where'd you say this Burakgazi guy was supposed to be again?"

"Cevahir Bedesteni. I guess they call it the Old Bazaar now." Halsey nodded up ahead, but they still weren't past enough of the tents and hanging tapestries for her to clearly identify the flashing silver sign she thought she'd seen. "Unfortunately, we can't get there today without taking the long way."

"Yeah, that's weird. You'd think the guy would've made it easier for us to find him."

"What, like set up shop at the entrance with a big-ass sign that says, 'Monster Hunters Needed, Apply Now'?"

Brigham laughed. "As cool as that would be, I was thinking about something a little more subtle. Closer to the center. Literally."

"I'm sure the contact has their reasons."

"Ha. Now you sound like Arthur." Brigham straightened his back and lifted his chin to make himself look particularly snobbish. He wobbled his head and flattened his voice in a surprisingly accurate impersonation of their uncle, who also happened to be the leader of the Ambrosius Council. "'Whatever our individual opinions may be, this Council as a whole has come to the unanimous conclusion that you two are the most fitting team for this particular mission. So you will answer the call.'"

After a wry laugh, Halsey adopted the pinched, nasally tone of their Aunt Beatrice and added, "'Well, I, for one, have no problem expressing my individual *opinion*. You were *not* my first choice. So be grateful to have any assignment at all, seeing as the rest of our militia still doesn't.'"

They both laughed at that, and Brigham fixed her with one of his winning grins. "That was actually pretty good."

"Yeah, thanks."

"No, I mean it, cuz. You'd make a mean Aunt Beatrice. Only not, you know, as mean as the real deal."

Halsey shook her head as she replayed the memory of her and her cousin standing in the Ambrosius Clan's Council room two days ago to receive the news about this particular mission. The cousins' playful mockery of said meeting was a fairly accurate portrayal of the way it had turned out, only with a fouler mood and a lot less smiling.

For the last two days, they'd planned their approach, sat through one incredibly boring briefing, and got the all-clear on their finalized travel arrangements to Istanbul. The Ambrosius Clan's A-Team had more than enough time to get used to being the first militia operatives sent on an active monster hunt since Halsey and her dad had returned to the Council with a bunch of severed ogre hands.

Plus, Halsey had used the time to put together a side mission of her own. Which she'd almost forgotten about amid the banter with her partner and best friend.

Now she was reminded of the extra effort needed to slip away from her cousin and make a pit stop before they met with the Turkish contact their Council had preemptively arranged for them.

Another flash of silver on her left caught her eye, and she glanced that way to find the source.

It took a lot of effort not to grin and dart away from her cousin when she saw the permanent sign hanging over a brick-and-mortar storefront. The design etched into the metal was different than she'd imagined it. Yet the image of a traditional Turkish double teapot and a tall, thin teacup with wavy lines rising from the top was as described to her.

To clarify further, the words "Iyi Çay" wafted beneath the shop's logo image, the letters curling around the edges of the sign like more tendrils of steam.

Damn it. I thought I'd have more time.

CHAPTER TWO

Halsey looked toward the tea shop and floundered for another conversational topic that would get her cousin as invested and distracted as she needed him to be.

"You know what still doesn't sit right with me, though?"

Brigham sniggered. "That's kind of a long list, Hal."

She ignored his joke and leaned toward him as she scanned the shops and stalls ahead. "The fact that the Council's apparently taking *requests* now."

"What? Come on." They swerved around a trio of teenage girls, two of whom eyed Brigham and giggled. Somehow, it went completely over his head. "That's old news at this point. We already figured that out in Ireland."

"No, Seamus Havalon *told* us in Ireland. This request didn't come from another Clan, Brigham. It came from some random normie in Turkey."

"Sure. As far as you know."

"Oh, right. On top of all the other things they refuse to tell us, our family Council's also keeping the identity of an entire elemental Clan hidden from *all* their operatives.

Makes total sense they'd send *us* on this mission to root out one more mind-blowing secret."

It seemed like that unlikely hypothetical of hers had Brigham completely stumped. Then he clicked his tongue and shrugged. "I don't know, man. There are weird sects all over the world that know all kinds of shit. That monsters exist. That magic's somewhere out there. That the Illuminati may or may not be a real thing…"

"Good one."

"Hey, I can neither confirm nor deny, right?" He laughed at what was obviously supposed to be a joke as he scanned the vendor stalls on their left. "Seriously, though, it makes sense that *someone* who isn't an elemental would know a few things about who we are and what we do. Not that any of them are nearly as prepared as they should be. Or that they actually know what they're doing when it comes to monsters. Hence, one random normie request sent to the Ambrosius Clan in Texas."

"Yeah, makes perfect sense." Halsey couldn't help but glance at the tea shop coming up on their right. *Talking's obviously not the right distraction today. Better hurry up and find what is.*

She opened her mouth with no idea what she was going to say next, but Brigham beat her to it.

"Look, if you're that worried about it, feel free to ask the guy. Who knows? Thoroughly vetting the dude in person might convince him we're as legit as we say."

She frowned. "What do you mean?"

"Really?" He swept a hand to indicate the entire bazaar. "Super public place. Obsessed with punctuality. Making us do all the work to get to *him* instead of, like... I don't know. Inviting us to his farm or something."

"Because everyone in Turkey has a farm."

"Or his house. Whatever." After rolling his eyes, Brigham mopped more sweat off his forehead and sighed. "Whoever reached out to the Council and asked for their best monster hunters, he's obviously not a hundred percent on board with the idea of anyone making this their full-time gig. So *us* being a little suspicious of *him* is the kinda thing an already suspicious dude would probably find appealing. I'm just sayin'."

"Huh." Halsey tilted her head, ran over what he'd said one more time, then shrugged. "I didn't even think about that."

"Which is why we're the A-Team, cuz." He grinned and nudged her. "Me and you. Brigham and Halsey. Brain and brawn—"

"Oh, you're saying I have no brain? Nice."

"Hey, you told me I have no pecs, so..."

"Well, maybe you should stop comparing yourself to every shirtless guy walking through the bazaar. Just sayin'."

"That's..." He pointed at her, paused, then clicked his tongue and looked away in defeat. "Shit, you're totally right. Moving on and speaking of the *maybe*-normie contact..."

"He's definitely a normie."

"TBD once we get there. Are you sure we're going the right way?"

Halsey scanned the crowd. A knot of urgent frustration tightened in her gut when she realized even though they'd been walking slowly, Iyi Çay was now behind them. She nodded ahead across what was still half of the entire bazaar. "We still gotta get all the way back there."

"Awesome." Brigham bobbed his head and stopped to examine a stall with hundreds of hats and leather belts hung on every inch of available wall space. "Hey, after we meet with this guy, you think we could come back through and do some actual shopping?"

She snorted and paused beside him. "Find something you like, cuz?"

"Kufi cap." He shot her a sidelong glance and wiggled his eyebrows. "I'm gettin' *vibes* from that blue one right up there."

Halsey pretended to look at her watch as she glanced across the walkway at the tea shop, then noticed the large mobile cobbler's stand rolling its rickety way toward them.

Has to be timed perfectly. I'm pretty good at timing. As long as he's as into the hat as he says.

"You know what? We'd still be a little early, even if we stopped for lunch."

Brigham turned away from the hats to stare at her. "Seriously?"

"Totally. I don't know about you, but I kinda got the impression punctuality was the top priority for this contact."

"Being early is usually a good thing…"

"Not by twenty minutes."

Now he looked confused. "Wait, you're not gonna tell me it's a bad idea?"

She frowned distractedly. "Why would I?"

"You know, some people think it's a religious thing. It's

not, though. It's more like a *style*. I looked it up. 'Cause, you know, those things are awesome."

Halsey nodded at the blue kufi. "Then go ahead and try it on."

"Hell, yeah."

Fortunately, their conversation had already caught the vendor's attention. He shuffled toward them with a beaming grin.

Brigham gestured toward the hat in question and spoke in short sentences, making it clear they were tourists without an ounce of applicable Turkish. While he did that, Halsey snuck another glance at the cobbler's cart headed toward them.

A little farther. Come on.

"That's it! Yes. Awesome." Brigham turned the hat in his hands, admiring the craftsmanship, then flipped it over once before placing it on his head with a hefty dose of Brigham flair. "Oh, *man*. Hit the Goldilocks zone on the first try!"

"The what?" She frowned at her cousin as he turned to face her.

"Seriously? The Goldilocks…shit, Hal. Not too big, not too small. Figured that one was a gimme."

"Right. Didn't know we were in the habit of comparing ourselves to nursery rhymes as grown adults, but my bad." He fixed her with a deadpan stare, and she scanned him, hoping her poker face was on-point today. The cobbler's cart had almost reached them. "Never thought I'd say this, either, but you look damn good in that kufi."

"Right?"

"Now you need a mirror." Halsey raised her hand to get

the hat vendor's attention. "Excuse me. Do you have a mirror so my cousin can take a look at himself?"

The man clearly didn't speak English, but Brigham was all over it.

"Mirror." He mimed looking at himself, using his hand as a substitute, smiling and nodding the whole time. "Do you have one?"

The vendor's eyes lit up. He nodded enthusiastically before spinning around to fulfill his customer's request.

"There you go, Hal." Brigham glanced over his shoulder and smirked. "That's the universal language right there. Charades."

"I thought it was supposed to be love. Or something sappy like that."

"Meh." He shrugged and turned back, already preening though he hadn't actually seen himself in the hat yet. "When all else fails, act it out. Simple."

"Or you could finally learn a second language," she murmured to keep him going as the cart drew closer.

"Yeah, I could. But anytime I go to a foreign country, *you're* right there with me. Problem solved. Except here, obviously. In Turkey, we're both swimming upstream. Not that I have a problem with that. We get by. If you stop to think about it, it sucks that almost every other country in the world speaks English 'cause they *have* to. We don't."

The cobbler's cart rumbled past the end of the hat vendor's long stall.

"I mean 'we' as in the whole country, though." Brigham nodded at the older man hobbling toward him with a tarnished hand mirror. "Obviously. Not *us*. Seriously, if we were regular normies who didn't have the whole elemental magic training *thing* to worry about in school, you think you'd still be fluent in..."

Halsey watched her cousin's back as she quickly stepped backward across the narrow walkway, crossing the open path two seconds before the cobbler's rickety cart passed where she'd been standing. Her timing couldn't have been more perfect.

Hinges held the sides of the handmade vehicle together where the planks of wood unfolded to create visual appeal for shoppers looking to have their shoes mended on the go. It was the perfect height to block all five feet, three inches of one young elemental. Whether or not the cobbler realized a young American woman was using his cart for a getaway, he didn't slow in his fervent push through the packed bazaar crowds.

Halsey didn't slow, either. She matched the man's pace perfectly, keeping the cart between herself and the other side of the walkway until she'd backtracked enough to reach Iyi Çay's propped-open front door.

She slipped inside, and the constant background noise of the hustling bazaar faded by a lot more than she'd expected with the door still open.

After peering over her shoulder to make sure she wasn't being followed by her own partner, Halsey tugged on her jacket lapels and turned her attention to the tea shop's interior.

She'd imagined what this rendezvous point would look like since before she and Brigham learned their first official mission was also conveniently in Turkey. Iyi Çay both did and did not match the images she'd held in her mind.

Of course, it *was* a tea shop. The metal patio tables and

chairs scattered across the main room made that clear. In the back was the counter, and behind that, a wall of floor-to-ceiling shelves housed enormous glass jars of loose-leaf teas beside packaged boxes meant for sale and private consumption. Several copper samovar teapots, different than the one depicted on the shop's front sign, had been laid out on the left side of the counter. Tendrils of steam rose from three of them. A neatly displayed collection of glass Turkish teacups with various accouterments on a silver tray rested beside the pots.

All told, the place was a tidy, mom-and-pop kind of store with low lighting and a lazily spinning overhead fan. A benign-looking meeting place.

What Halsey didn't expect was to find groups of three to four men occupying almost every table inside the shop. All of them were nearing the end of middle age or had recently passed it. No one spoke, and while every patron of Iyi Çay had a teacup in front of him, that clearly wasn't their main focus.

At least a dozen gazes settled on Halsey as she headed for the counter. She smiled in greeting at the first few but quickly gave up when all she got in return were unchanging stares and deep scowls perpetually set in wrinkled faces.

Okay... Feels like we're only missing a few chessboards and a box of Cuban cigars.

The thought almost made her laugh, but she stuffed her amusement under a serious, businesslike mask. If the older gentlemen passing their late-morning hours inside Iyi Çay had any inkling of who she was and why she was here, they didn't show it.

Gotta make this quick. And efficient. Still plenty of time 'til we have to meet our official contact, but if Brigham finds me before I'm done...

She didn't want to think about that because acting desperate wouldn't do much to back her up here. Not with this.

Unfortunately, no one stood behind the counter to dutifully tend to new customers. There was no bell to ring or any other way to get an employee's attention. She could've knocked on the counter or shouted through the cracked-open door in the back corner, but she wouldn't be *that* person.

She had to do this right.

Instead, she wandered along the counter to study the samovar teapots wafting steam and an attractive combination of scents into the air. The sign cards laid out in front of them were written in Turkish, but the small drip trays showed color variations of rich brown, light red, pink, and a washed-out yellow-green.

I could probably get a nice, dark black tea outta one of these when I'm done. No doubt it's the real deal here.

As soon as the thought occurred, slow, clunky footsteps sounded from behind the door in the corner. By the time Halsey looked up from the teapots, the owner of those footsteps had emerged and headed her way.

He was enormous.

If this is Aydem, I'm gonna have to rethink everything I knew about record-keepers being cranky, shriveled old men.

CHAPTER THREE

The bald man with a mountain of muscle beneath every square inch of skin behind the counter didn't seem surprised to see Halsey in his store. He didn't exactly look happy about it, either. He fixed her with the same dubious scowl as the other men seated at the tables, though he had to be at least fifteen years younger than his clientele. Halsey started to think that might have been the only difference between them until the giant guy spoke.

Most likely, it was a grumbled greeting in Turkish. Part of her wished she'd spent more time in the region and picked up a welcoming phrase or two. Then, it would've been easier to distinguish between a grumpy "How can I help you" and something a lot less inviting.

At least he's acknowledging me. So here we go.

Halsey put on her best "maybe you can help me" smile and sidled down the counter until she and the six-and-a-half-foot giant met in the middle. She casually leaned forward and announced, "Hi. I'm here to see Aydem."

The giant dude studied her without expression, then pointed at the samovar teapots. "Tea."

"Yes, I know. Some of the best, by the smell of it." She glanced over her shoulder, partially to make sure Brigham still hadn't found her but mostly to gauge the elderly patrons' reactions. They were all still staring at her. Only one of them moved to slurp his dark, muddy-looking tea without looking away.

Okay, now I'm starting to wonder if these guys are permanent fixtures here.

It was harder to keep smiling at the giant man, but she managed well enough under the circumstances. "The friend of mine who recommended this place also said I could find Aydem here. Or at least someone who can point me in the right direction."

Now it was Big Guy's turn to cast a sweeping glance across the tea shop's front room, hitting every gentleman's face along the way. When he looked back at Halsey, he sighed through his nose in agitation and pointed at the teapots again. "You don't want tea?"

She pressed her lips together and tried not to sound like a jerk when she replied, "Maybe after I talk to Aydem."

"Only tea here. You don't want tea, you don't stay here. Go."

She chuckled wryly and lowered her voice to a murmur. "Wow. You're really not gonna help me out on this one, are you?"

"I can help with tea."

"Yeah, we've established that." With time on the talking mountain's side instead of hers, Halsey's ability to remain quiet and patient gave out. "Let's try something else."

She sidestepped toward the steaming silver pots and the glass teacups beside them, but what she really wanted was the silver tray laden with napkins, a honey jar, lemon slices, and metal spoons. She grabbed the tray, slid it noisily across the counter, then pulled the spoons from the colorfully painted jar that held them.

Before she could perform the next step of her slight improvisation, Big Guy slapped a hand on the counter and caught Halsey's wrist with the other in a hot, achingly tight grip.

She froze, neither fighting back nor giving in as the man leaned over the counter.

He raised an eyebrow. "Stealing. Not a good idea."

"I like to think of it more as bartering." She held his gaze as she replied.

In the same moment, Halsey reached out with her elemental magic to the inherent life force in all metal, even a handful of well-used, slightly tarnished teaspoons. It responded instantly to her call. Even if she hadn't been holding the giant man's gaze to make her point, she wouldn't need to look down to know her magic was working. She could feel it.

She heard it, too. A clanging *plink* rose from the silver tray she'd pulled toward her, followed instantly by another. And another.

She tightened her hold on the spoons, which grew smaller as, one by one, they morphed into large, heavy, pure gold nuggets.

Before Big Guy could blink, the last of the spoons shrank and hardened in her hand before spilling from her closed fist onto the silver tray. The whole process lasted about five seconds and made more than enough noise for every tea shop patron to have heard something unbelievable happening.

It was enough to make the giant bald man with his hand clamped around her wrist a believer. He dipped his head before drawing his gaze to the silver tray.

When she opened her fist again, the guy released her.

"I'd like to see Aydem now," she murmured. "Please and thank you."

Big Guy grunted and grabbed the tray off the counter with one hand. He looked her over one more time, then sighed. "Wait."

He turned and walked across the narrow strip between the counter and the shelves, heading for the back room.

All right, then. I had to play my wild card earlier than I'd expected, but at least he takes me seriously now. And Aydem will too. I hope.

Using alchemy to get a private chat with a contact wasn't exactly protocol, especially in front of an audience. Still, this was a private side trip, not part of any official mission. She was willing to let a few things slide. Not that she'd been a major fan of following protocol anyway.

She drummed her fingers on the countertop and waited for what felt like an eternity with only the sounds of old men slurping their tea and the constant buzz of the ceiling fan. When she looked over her shoulder again, the men still stared at her with unchanged expressions. One of them sitting at the closest table motioned toward the samovar teapots and nodded.

"Help myself?" She gestured between herself and the tea, and two others nodded. "Well, thanks."

Technically, I paid for several cups of tea and more than a few sets of spoons. Don't mind if I do.

Halsey returned to the tall, curvy pewter teapots, grabbed a cup, and took her time trying to decipher the flavors. She really didn't want to finish her complimentary drink before Big Guy returned and grumbled, "Come on back."

As she settled on the darkest tea, figuring it would have the most caffeine, heavy footsteps pounded past the shop's open door. They stopped, then slowly returned.

"You gotta be shittin' me," a familiar voice snapped.

Halsey froze, her hand outstretched toward the teapots. It was Brigham.

Damn it. Why can't people deliver a message without having to fight me on it?

"Halsey, what the hell?" He stormed across the shop, making it impossible to keep pretending she hadn't heard him.

She spun with a tight smile plastered across her face and raised the empty glass teacup toward him. "Check it out… Oh, hey. You got the hat."

"Yeah, I got the *hat*." Her cousin stopped in front of her, then glanced over his shoulder at the staring old men silently drinking their tea. "Then you were gone, and I almost tore this place apart looking for you. What were you thinking?"

"That I…wanted some tea?"

"Badly enough to ditch me in the middle of a bazaar purchase, huh? Since when do you drink tea?"

"Since being in Turkey. It's kind of a big deal here, in case you haven't noticed."

"You know what's a big deal here?" Brigham spat, then lowered his voice and leaned closer. "Leaving me high and dry like that, man. That's *never* part of the deal—"

"Hey, relax. Okay? You were doing your thing at the hat stand. I'm sorry, but watching you fall in love with your own reflection isn't my idea of a fun way to spend an extra half-hour before our meeting."

The second she said it, Halsey regretted the way it had come out. That was *before* her cousin blinked, stepped back, and fixed her with a hurt look.

"What's going on with you today?" he murmured. "You're all over the place. Literally and figuratively."

"I'm fine." *I'm just keeping secrets from my partner, 'cause this one definitely takes the crazy-cake.*

"You mean you don't wanna tell me." Brigham nodded. "Fine. Don't tell me on our way to the *meeting* we have with our *contact*. You know, the guy you said was more concerned about punctuality than knowing anything else about us. Remember that part?"

"Funny."

"Well, it wasn't supposed to be. Come on. Put that down. We gotta go." He nodded at the empty glass in her hand, then half-spun toward the open door.

Halsey pressed her lips together and turned back to the teapots. "I haven't had my tea yet."

"Dude."

She reached for the spigot again, her mind racing. *He's gonna be on me like a sheepdog after this. Unless I can figure out how to get him out of here for another ten minutes. That's all I need...*

"It's supposed to be really good," she told him casually

as she turned the spigot and let the tea burble into her cup. "Try it with me. You never know, cuz. Could be the best thing you've ever—"

The back corner door banged against the interior wall, and out stepped Big Guy again. He barked something in Turkish that sounded a lot less inviting than his previous growl. He no longer seemed like a giant, bald, terminally bored owner or even an employee.

He looked pissed.

"Maybe it's not a self-service thing," Brigham muttered.

"No, it's definitely—shit." She'd forgotten to turn off the spigot. She did so now, suffering only a small burn from a few drops on her hand. Most of the excess had splattered all over the tile floor at her feet. "Sorry," she called toward Big Guy with a tight smile. "I'll clean this up. You have a rag or something I can—"

"Who is he?" the man interrupted gruffly. "Hat man."

Brigham raised his eyebrows and tried not to look too happy about it. "Hey, I kinda like the sound of that. Hat man..."

"No clue," Halsey blurted.

"What?" Her cousin gaped at her.

Big Guy grunted. "Americans. Who is he?"

"Hey, just because we're from the same place doesn't mean we *know* each other." Feigning surprise and insult, she faced Brigham as she set the overflowing teacup on the counter. "Get some tea or don't, man. I really don't care. Let me finish what I'm doing in here, okay? Starting with..." She shuffled along the counter, trying to peer over it in search of something she could use to clean up the mess. "A rag. I'll even use a mop if you want. If you have one. I'm not trying to walk in here and make things worse for you or…anybody else."

Damn it, I was so close to sitting down with this guy. Played hardball and everything. Perfectly. Now I'm playing class clown in a foreign country. Come on!

She hoped the giant bald dude got the message behind that. Yet whether he did or not didn't matter because Big Guy folded his arms and sneered at her. "Out."

"Really? It's only a little spill." Halsey glanced at the rather large tea puddle on the floor. "Like I said, I'm happy to clean it up if you'll *give me the chance*—"

"I don't like him." Big Guy jerked his chin toward Brigham. "I don't like the hat."

"But…" She laughed tensely and leaned away from the counter, wishing telepathy was included in the mixed bag of elemental powers she'd inherited from generations of Ambrosiuses before her. "I thought we had an understanding."

"I speak English. No more understanding. Get out."

Yeah, he's not budging. Now I can't even argue my case because my amazing partner *is way too good at finding me when I sneak off.*

Halsey gritted her teeth, spread her arms, and slowly backed away from the counter. "All right. Got it. I'll try again another time—"

"And I will throw you out another time." The giant man snorted. He turned his intimidating stare on Brigham.

"Hal." Brigham's smile was so tight she could hear it in his voice. "Time to go."

Her frustrated growl was the only response she could manage that wouldn't get her literally thrown out. As she turned, she glanced at Big Guy, searching for any sign that his decision to turn her away completely and indefinitely was for show because Brigham had joined them. She found nothing.

The man behind the counter let them get halfway across the shop before barking, "It is stealing if you do not pay."

"Pay?" Halsey spun and scowled at him. "For *what?*"

The corner of his mouth twitched as he gestured toward the dangerously full cup on the counter. "You wanted tea."

"I didn't even drink it."

He glanced at the floor. "And the spill."

She rolled her eyes and addressed her cousin. "You have any change?"

"Seriously?" Brigham darted a glance at Big Guy, then stared at her. "You walked in here without any money to pay for your *tea?*"

"No, but I only have large bills," she grumbled. "I'm pretty sure this guy isn't gonna give me any change."

"Aw, for the love of…" Brigham fished out a handful of coins from his pocket and flicked through it, shaking his head. "How much is a stupid cup of tea?"

"That's good. Thanks." Halsey snatched it all from his palm and marched back toward the counter.

Big Guy didn't move. None of the old men said a word as they enjoyed their hot morning drinks along with the rare, highly entertaining show from two clueless foreigners.

I'll be back, Halsey vehemently thought as she held Big Guy's unflinching gaze. *Or I'll figure out another way to get my ten minutes with Aydem. Hopefully without this goon around.*

Instead of walking up to the man, she snatched the full glass from the counter. Steam still rose from the tea, and it was absolutely hot enough to scald anyone.

Anyone but an elemental.

Halsey called on the air around her and the water within the tea, commanding both together to cool the drink before angrily raising the cup to her lips. Her magic had worked, but due to either her frustration or the fact that she was using it to spite the giant, it didn't work nearly as much as she'd wanted it to.

The tea burned all the way down, but she couldn't stop now.

She knocked back the entire cup of dark red-brown, achingly hot tea like it was a pint of beer. The empty glass clinked back on the counter, followed by the jingle and clack of Brigham's spare change as she slapped it down in front of Big Guy. Glaring at him, she swallowed the heat still burning its way into her stomach and murmured, "Your tea is delicious."

She whipped her hand off the counter, sending two small lyra coins spinning away, and stormed across the shop toward the open door.

Brigham looked back and forth between his cousin and the mean-looking muscle behind the counter, though the bald man's scowl had morphed into a smirk. When he realized Halsey wasn't waiting for him, he nodded at Big Guy, then spun to follow her out.

CHAPTER FOUR

As soon as she was clear of Iyi Çay's walls, Halsey stopped alongside the bazaar's narrow walkway. She stuck her hands on her hips and gave herself permission to feel the rawness of her throat as she thoroughly berated herself for botching her one chance for a secret meeting she really needed with a Turkish man she'd never met. Or even seen, which was also a massive bummer.

"Was it really that good?" Brigham muttered behind her. "'Cause now I'm kinda feeling like trying some tea."

"Yeah." She sighed, rolled her shoulders back, and waited for him to catch up. "I probably won't taste anything for a week now, but I guess it was worth it."

"Okay…" He inspected her, then gestured down the walkway. "So you got tea, and I got a hat. Can we get back to our regularly scheduled program now? Or is there something else on your secret wish list of things to try in Turkey that I should know about?"

Oh, man, he's gonna be pissed when I tell him what I was

trying to do. If *I tell him*. 'Cause if I don't talk to Aydem, there won't be anything to tell.

"No." She managed a small smile before brushing her hair away from the sides of her face. "That was it."

"Great." Brigham didn't look convinced, but he was more concerned with making it to their meeting and kicking off their actual mission than questioning his partner any further. He clapped a hand on Halsey's shoulder and gave her a little shake. "Then we're good. As long as you're not about to tell me our rendezvous has moved elsewhere."

She snorted. "Not as far as I know."

"Awesome." He started in the original direction they'd been heading, then stopped and sighed in irritation before pulling his phone from his back pocket. "Now I jinxed myself. Put the idea in my own head, so I'm double-checking emails. Hang tight a sec."

"Yeah, okay." Halsey chuckled and waited for her cousin to go through the motions of checking and re-checking that they had all their militia I's dotted and T's crossed. Brigham had been a stickler for details as long as she'd known him, which was forever. Yet, in the last few months, his habit of gathering concrete facts and double-checking his work had leaned more toward paranoia.

Makes sense when the last few months have unraveled everything we thought we knew about monsters. Which sucks, 'cause that's the kinda thing we were born needing to know.

The bustling noise and flashing colors of Istanbul's culture and people were too much to ignore, even while standing in the middle of the bazaar as her partner reassured himself of the mission specifics. Halsey folded her arms and looked past her cousin at Iyi Çay's entrance. She couldn't see inside from here, but the glinting silver sign above the door was clear enough.

I'll figure something else out. The guy's in there, that's for sure. He can't spend all his time holed up in a tea shop. I need to figure out where else to meet him before we wrap up this mission. Lucky for me, it's been pretty slow going so far.

Movement and a dark patch of color caught her eye from the depression by the open front door. A second later, a man in a slate-gray jacket and dark jeans emerged from Iyi Çay.

At first glance, nothing stood out about him. However, she soon realized this man was much younger than any of the patrons sitting at the tables inside. She and Brigham hadn't been out of the shop long enough for anyone to enter, make a purchase, and leave again. Not with the way Big Guy liked to take his time with his job.

This man with the closely shaved hair must have been in the back with Big Guy and could be Aydem. That seemed like a probable explanation. Then she noticed something that drowned out all the hustling noise and the energy of the people around her.

On the back of the man's shaved head, beneath the base of his skull, was a dark, blood-red tattoo roughly half the size of Halsey's palm.

At first, she thought it was the same blood rune as the ones she and her dad found on the ogre hands almost a month ago.

No, not exactly the same.

The thought mixed with the sight of the tattoo as time seemed to slow, almost hypnotizing her. She couldn't say *why* that mark looked so much like the blood runes other than the color and the similarity of the patterns. She didn't even know what other blood runes might look like because she'd only ever seen the one.

That didn't seem to matter. Something inside her screamed that the tattoo, and the man himself, were somehow tied to blood magic.

There was no way to prove it. Not unless she ran after him and tackled him in the center of a highly public, incredibly crowded bazaar.

She considered it until the man turned in her direction to scan the narrow walkway. Even if it had occurred to her to stop staring, she couldn't.

The man caught sight of her. His dark eyes widened, then he turned and headed in the opposite direction. Halsey got another glimpse of the tattoo before he pulled the cotton hood of his dark jacket over his head.

Like he recognized me. Which is totally impossible, but... If he's a blood human or tied to some kind of remnant cult, what the hell was he doing in there? Hot anger pulsed through her, and she sprinted after him anyway. *Aydem's supposed to be on* our *side.*

"Damn it, Hal!" Brigham's shout ripped her from her single-minded focus a split second before his hand clamped around her upper arm, and he yanked her to a halt. "I look at my phone for a whole sixty seconds, and you're gone again!"

"It's the..." She searched the crowd for the man in the dark hood, but he'd completely disappeared. "There was a..."

How the hell am I supposed to explain that now without telling him I made a secret pseudo-appointment?

"You know, I like it a lot better when *I'm* the one who goes off track, and *you're* the one who pulls me back to center." Brigham hauled her to his side and frowned, one hundred percent serious this time. "And yeah, I'm being literal right now. What are you *doing*?"

"I..." She looked over her shoulder to double-check that she hadn't missed anything. "I thought I saw something."

"Something more important than us sitting down with our contact and *doing our jobs*?" They skirted around a group of people studying a stall. "I swear. It's like you're in a totally different world today. If that's the case, you need to tell me right now."

"What?"

"See?"

Halsey shook her head as they made their way through the crowd toward the far end of the bazaar. "No. I'm here. Promise."

He studied her, then nodded. "Good." He slid his fingers along the brim of his newly purchased hat. "Listen, I get being a little distracted sometimes. Obviously. But if I look away for five seconds and you're gone again, I'm gonna have to call it. As in we fail our mission. Got that?"

"Brigham—"

"'Cause even if I *could* do this alone, Hal, I sure as hell don't want to."

"I got it!" Her shout came out louder than she'd intended, surprising them both. Yet they kept walking because they did have somewhere else to be. "I'm sorry, Brigham."

"Huh. An apology right off the bat."

She shot him a sidelong glance and saw the beginnings of a smile flicker across his lips. "Yeah. There's no point trying to explain, anyway. I let my curiosity run away with the show. It won't happen again."

"At least not on *this* mission, right?" Brigham sniggered, and it broke the tension building between them. "We both know the second we're done with this thing in Turkey and head home, your curiosity's gonna be the *only* thing driving this boat."

"Ha. Well, we still have plenty of unanswered questions about…everything. So yeah." She bumped her shoulder against his and chuckled. "Don't worry. I'll let you off at the first stop."

"So you can have all the fun by yourself? I don't think so."

She was smiling again, but she couldn't stop thinking about the guy with the blood-red tattoo who'd looked at her like they were supposed to know each other.

Big Guy back there didn't think it was weird seeing a bunch of spoons transformed into gold. If a regular dude like that is used to seeing magic, maybe I was supposed to know who Tattoo is. And if any of the cowards in our family had manned up enough to show their "best team" how to recognize a blood rune in the modern world, I wouldn't feel like I've stepped into one hell of a snare.

The thought that she might have given something away in her attempts to be careful this time, especially keeping things from her cousin, sent a shiver across Halsey's shoulders despite the mid-August heat. Her light canvas jacket came in handy in a moment like this, but even as she slid her hands into her pockets, it didn't offer the warm hug of relief she'd expected.

Today, she carried an extra secret. She was instantly reminded of it as her fingers brushed the cool, smooth surface of the baseball-sized copper sphere in her pocket.

After Ireland, she'd promised Brigham she would leave the thing safely tucked away at home until they could figure out what it was and what they were supposed to do with it. Safely. Together.

Yet the copper orb she'd impossibly transmuted from a mound of leftover magical sand was her ticket to getting the answer she needed from Aydem. Unless the meeting with him in Iyi Çay was only a setup for one brutally determined Ambrosius.

No. I don't care how much has changed. She wouldn't have given me his name if she had any idea I'd be compromised.

She tried to reassure herself of this as she and Brigham finally reached the far end of the bazaar, close to their rendezvous with the contact who was effectively a rare "client" of the Ambrosius Clan militia. However, she wasn't completely sure of anything anymore. That had been the problem for the last three months.

CHAPTER FIVE

One month earlier...
"Oh. It's only you?" Greta Ambrosius peered through the cracked-open door of her private bungalow in the middle of the enormous Ambrosius family estate property, then shrugged. "Well, I hope you're not expecting cookies and milk this time."

Halsey couldn't help but laugh at her grandmother. "That's definitely a Brigham thing. I *would* settle for one of your famous grilled cheeses, though."

"Huh. I bet you would." The woman smirked and stepped aside to let her granddaughter in. Her bright blue eyes shimmered in the sunlight spilling through the front door.

Halsey returned the knowing smile, stepped through the front door, and looked around. "You know, the last time I was here, I thought I'd officially lost my mind."

"Welcome to every day of my life for the last twenty years, girl. Give or take a few."

"If you feel like you're crazy for twenty years straight, wouldn't that mean…"

"That you're actually batshit nuts?" Greta sniggered as she shoved the door shut, then dusted off her hands. "I ask myself the same question at least once a day, kid. Sometimes more. Something tells me you didn't come here to talk about how crazy I think *I* am on a regular basis, though."

"Not really, no."

"Okay, then." Greta grinned and led her granddaughter to the bungalow's living room. There, she plopped on the couch and waited for Halsey to join her.

After Halsey kicked off her shoes and climbed into the old, tattered, faded green armchair that had belonged to her Pappy, she pulled her feet up and crossed them beneath her. "So."

"So." Her grandmother leaned back, threw an arm over the armrest, and crossed one leg over the other. "How was Ireland? The second time, I mean."

"You assume we've already been out there and back since the last time I stopped by?"

"Ten days ago? Absolutely." Greta laughed and tilted her head. "You did *go*, didn't you?"

"Yeah. We went." Despite her efforts to the contrary, Halsey couldn't help another smile. "You were right. Going back to *the source* of it all did help with a few things. Brigham might not say the same, but I honestly don't think Brigham knows what happened out there."

"As in, you doubt the full capacity of his comprehension levels, or you're being an ass and not telling him everything?"

Halsey's jaw dropped open in surprise as she stared at her grandmother. "You really think I'd try to hide things from my own partner?"

"Partner. Cousin. Best friend." Greta shrugged. "Truth is, girl, that part's in your blood too. Whether you like it or not. I know I'm your favorite, but I could make your head spin with how many things I've kept to myself over the years instead of spilling my guts to the whole damn family."

Halsey nestled back and decided to face her grandmother's tendency to go for the shock factor first head-on. "Make my head spin, huh? You mean like how, once upon a time, the Havalon Clan reached out to ask our family for help with a serious monster problem, and *you* were the only one who bothered to answer their call?"

Greta looked stunned. Then she threw her head back and howled with laughter, her silver hair swinging away from her face like a chin-length curtain. When she settled down enough to speak, she wagged a finger at her granddaughter. "So you *did* see them. Fantastic choice, by the way. And now I—" She laughed again and shook her head. "I really have to know how the hell you got Cillian to agree to a meeting."

"Uh... By showing up on his doorstep, actually."

"Isn't *that* interesting?" Greta tried to imagine the scene, then nodded. "Well, I guess if you're gonna go all-in, that's the way to do it. What did they do, offer the option to pop by for a chat and a pint?"

Halsey dipped her head at the memory of their short but incredibly exciting—not to mention almost deadly—few days in Ireland with the elemental Havalon Clan.

"Believe it or not, Brigham's insane thoroughness made the whole Clan think we were screwing with them. They weren't even gonna reply, but Cillian's son wanted to know if a person like Brigham actually existed. And me, I guess."

"Cillian's son." A slow smile crept across the older woman's face. "What did young Seamus think when he found you were, in fact, real?"

He hit on me every chance he got...

Halsey snorted. She wouldn't mind talking to her grandmother about Seamus since Greta Ambrosius was probably the only person in the family who would make that conversation fun and judgment-free. However, Halsey hadn't come here to talk about nonexistent flings with elementals who lived halfway across the world.

"He invited us to dinner with the Council," she replied instead. "I gotta say the Havalons' Council meetings are a hell of a lot more fun than ours."

That got her grandmother cracking up all over again, most likely because the woman understood how true that was.

Since the subject of the Havalon Clan had been brought up, Halsey realized she had to give Greta at least a brief, broad-picture summary of her and Brigham's trip to the Emerald Isle. Meeting with Seamus and the rest of the Havalon family, the other Clan's openness to Halsey's theory about the Mother of Monsters' return causing so much chaos. The stories from superstitious normies about monsters, moving shadows, and ghostly figures in the night. And, of course, the werewolf hunt.

Greta looked particularly interested in the silverback alpha *speaking* to Halsey in the rocky clearing before he forced her to end his life so he wouldn't end hers first. However, she didn't look surprised.

When Halsey realized her grandmother wasn't thrown by even the most unbelievable parts of the story, it was easier to think she'd come to the right place for the information she needed. Again.

"Sounds like you did the right thing," Greta claimed after a moment of consideration. "He wanted to die, you wanted to live, so it was cause and effect. Don't let it get to you."

Halsey leaned back against the headrest. "Well, it's a little too late for that."

"Maybe that'll change. Most things do, given enough time."

They sat in silence for a moment longer, then Halsey had to start asking the real questions. "Any idea what it means?"

"What's that?"

"*Munkurinn hafdi rétt fyrir sér.*" She repeated the alpha werewolf's last words.

"Hmm." Greta stroked her chin, then shrugged. "Sound pre-Germanic, if you ask me."

"Yeah, Seamus said Icelandic. Or Old Norse, which would be insane."

Her grandmother's eyes widened. "*Would* it? Most of us would call an alpha werewolf *begging* you to kill him pretty insane, too."

Halsey snorted. "True. What about the name? Rolfr Orgnussen."

"You're asking me like I know a lot of werewolves' names, girl."

"Well, you never know with *you*. Figured I'd check."

They both laughed, then Greta grew serious again as she considered the implications. "You think he was talking about the Matriarch."

"It makes sense. That alpha was there the night Brigham and I found the silver coffin. It hit home when he kept talking about how he'd already put her away, but now she's back."

"That does tend to skew one's perception of the whole thing."

"It sounds a hell of a lot like he was talking about the Mother of Monsters. I need to figure out who he really was so I can prove it."

"Obviously." Greta fixed her granddaughter with a knowing look as she pondered the idea. "I also can't help but notice you referring to this silverback alpha as *he* instead of *it*."

Halsey blinked in surprise. "Because he was a man. At the end, at least."

"Aren't they all?" With a shrug and a wistful sigh, the older woman gazed at the ceiling and bobbed her head as she gathered her thoughts around the conversation. It reminded Halsey of Brigham when he tried to put whatever crazy thing she'd told him into a nice, neat, logical little box. With Meemaw, that look meant something different.

Great. Now she's going to say something so ridiculously profound that it ends up sounding like a crazy old lady's ranting. Until it starts to make sense later when I actually need it. Though it won't make sense right now.

Greta snapped her fingers and smiled. "If I were you,

girl, I'd go in search of a few more records. They're harder to find and not nearly as reliable since they tend to change with the times, but you never know what you might drum up."

The soundness of her grandmother's thoughts surprised Halsey. "More records. You mean like in the Clan library? I'm pretty sure Charlemagne banned me for life, and it's gonna take a lot more than 'please and thank you' to get him to—"

"Ha!" Greta slapped her thigh. "You think our *family* has the only existing records of where monsters come from? Where *we* come from? Think again. You'll have to go ask in person, though."

"Ask…who?"

"The records, girl. *Living* records. I can point you in the right direction if you like. The rest is up to you. Assuming our dear, thickheaded, blind-as-shit family doesn't decide to start doubling down on missions for the Alpha Hunter."

Halsey balked at hearing the Havalons' new name for her coming from her grandmother's mouth. "Did you already talk to Cillian about this?"

"I know things you can't possibly imagine, kiddo." Greta fluttered a hand as if she were revealing a cool new magic trick. "Even if I told you *how* I know them, you wouldn't believe me."

Halsey narrowed her eyes and surveyed her grandmother. "It's Fiona. You're still in touch with Fiona."

The older woman smiled before she changed the subject again. "Things are gonna change for you, girl. In a big way. They changed for me like this once. Don't make the same mistake I did."

Holy shit. Are we really going down that road right now?

Halsey swallowed and forced herself to tread carefully. "What mistake is that?"

"Putting the Clan's orders above what you *know* to be true." Greta sighed and rolled her eyes. "I let them push me out because I thought it would open their eyes. Now I realize what I *should* have done, and I'm telling you right now to do the same. Don't stop until you're in the ground."

"Damn, Meemaw." Their shared laugh was tense and tinged with regret.

Until I'm in the ground, huh? Maybe she can help me figure the rest of it out before it comes to that.

"What's that about?" Greta asked.

"What?"

"That look on your face. Like your best friend asked you to pet-sit their iguana for a week, and now you have to tell them the damn thing died on you."

Halsey choked back a laugh and shook her head. "That's not funny."

"Of course it is. If you can't laugh at the morbid shit, girl, nothing else in the world is gonna hit the spot for humor. Not when you have *our* job."

"True. Mostly, I was trying to imagine Brigham with a pet iguana."

Greta wrinkled her nose, then squeezed her eyes shut. "Let's table that image for another time."

"Deal."

"Now you can tell me what else is on your mind." The woman raised an eyebrow at her granddaughter, then swung her legs onto the couch cushions to sprawl sideways. "Hit me." She pointed a warning finger at Halsey and added, "Keep in mind that if you decide to take that literally, I *always* hit back."

"Noted." Halsey slid her hands into her jacket pockets and puffed out a sigh.

Might as well get it over with now. What's the worst she can do? Tell me to go find some living records? If she takes any of this to the Council, neither one of us will get the answers we want. But it's Meemaw.

Her fingers curled around the cool, rounded metal of the copper sphere she'd been keeping in her jacket. She slowly withdrew the transmuted object made of insanely powerful magic and sand. "This is what I came here to ask you about."

They both studied the copper orb for what felt like forever. At last, Halsey pried her gaze away from it to gauge her grandmother's reaction.

Greta didn't *have* a reaction at first. She continued lounging against the armrest like she didn't have a care in the world. Then she tilted her head and snorted. "Well, now I'm relieved."

"I can explain how I—wait. You're what?"

"Relieved. Yes. That's exactly the word I was looking for. At least, I think it is."

Halsey frowned. "I don't buy it."

"You really thought you could walk into my house with that insanely powerful magic flowing off you in waves, and I *wouldn't* notice?" The woman chuckled. "I thought maybe something happened to you in Ireland."

"Meemaw, I told you what happened to me in Ireland."

"Oh, you told me what you *did*, sure. Nothing *happened* to you, though. I wasn't gonna say anything at first. You know, in case my granddaughter having her magic transmuted by something she doesn't understand, maybe without her knowing it, turned out to be a touchy subject."

Halsey nearly dropped the copper orb. "*My* magic."

"Then you pull out *this* thing, which is obviously the source of all that transmuted energy, so yes. I think 'relieved' is the word I want." Greta pushed upright and nodded at the sphere. "Can I see it?"

"Holy shit," Halsey whispered before releasing a breathless laugh. "You almost gave me a heart attack."

"Don't be so dramatic." The woman clapped her hands and opened them like they were on a basketball court. "Give it here."

After a brief pause, Halsey lobbed the orb across the living room, and her grandmother snatched it from the air.

Greta's eyes widened as her fingers clamped around the cool metal. She chuckled and turned the thing over in her hands. "Now, where the hell did you find *this*?"

"Well, technically…I made it."

"You…" She turned her head and shook the copper orb by her ear as if listening for something inside. "There's obviously something you're not telling me, girl."

"Yeah, obviously. I haven't had the chance yet."

Her grandmother laughed, then slumped against the couch cushions like a teenager and tossed the orb high above her head. Halsey almost leapt from her armchair when the copper orb shot toward the ceiling and again when Greta didn't move to catch the thing until the last minute. The heavy weight of condensed metal and magic slapping into the woman's palm was a small relief.

"Meemaw?"

"Uh-huh?" Greta drew her arm back in preparation for another toss.

Halsey sucked in a sharp breath, jerked her feet out from under her, and slapped them on the floor, ready to jump up and retrieve the magical item. "Could you not—"

"What's that?"

"Could you not play catch with that thing?" She managed to say it softly, then sighed and added, "Please?"

"You think it's fragile?"

"I don't know *what* to think about it. Honestly, I'd rather not push it."

"Huh. Fair enough." Greta shrugged and took a moment longer to study the orb. "Think fast."

Halsey lurched from the chair when her grandmother sent the sphere flying across the room. Only Greta hadn't thrown the thing *at* her granddaughter.

The orb whizzed toward the opposite corner of the living room. Though Halsey knew there was no way she could catch it, she still shouted in surprise and reached for it.

The copper sphere stopped midair and hovered like it had been caught by an invisible hand.

She froze and couldn't stop staring at the thing.

"Hmm." Greta folded her arms. "Interesting."

"Are you doing this?" Halsey whispered.

"Hey, I only threw it. The rest is all you, kid."

"No, it's not." Halsey struggled to breathe as she tried to wrap her mind around what had happened. Magic, obviously. Except not the kind she'd been using her entire life.

Her grandmother chuckled. "Why's that? It's a big ball of copper—"

"Yeah, but I didn't even call to it!" The outburst seemed to return her full awareness, and she slowly lowered her outstretched hand. The copper sphere stayed where it was. Halsey drew in a slightly shaky breath. "That wasn't my elemental magic, Meemaw. I didn't call to the metal. I was... Like when you see a vase start to fall off the mantelpiece, and you know you're too far away to catch it, but you reach for it anyway."

"Ah." Greta looked between her granddaughter's confused stiffness and the hovering sphere. "You mean like the old vase you and your cousin knocked off *that* mantelpiece?"

Halsey glanced at the shelf in question above the living room fireplace, and the rest of the memory came back to her. "Yep. Like that one. Which, by the way, was totally Brigham's fault. *I'm* the one who tried to stop it. In case he never actually copped to it."

"Ha! Of course he did. That boy couldn't keep a secret if his life depended on it, so I do hope it never does. You're wrong, though."

"No, I was there. It was a long time ago, but trust me. I remember—"

Greta blew a raspberry and shook her head. "I don't give a shit about the vase, girl. I'm saying you're wrong about *that*."

Halsey followed her grandmother's gaze to the hovering orb. "You clearly know something I don't, because I only...reacted."

"First of all, I know *so* many things you don't. In the future, you can simply assume that's the case."

The young elemental chuckled as she stared at the

transmuted orb. The tingling feeling of dread that had raced across her whole body was fading now, and she started to feel like herself again.

"Second of all, you absolutely know what this is. You only haven't realized it yet."

"Meemaw, how would I—"

"Because you already said it, girl." Greta cleared her throat and thrust a finger in the air as she made a laughable attempt at impersonating her granddaughter. "'That wasn't my elemental magic, Meemaw.'" She grinned and threw up her other pointer finger. "'I only...reacted.'"

"Okay, now you're mocking me."

"Maybe a little." The woman dropped her arms and nodded. "You did say it best. I don't think this was your *elemental* magic, either."

"That's the only kind I have."

"Obviously not. Don't ask me what else it could be because I have no fucking clue. I'm as surprised as you are. Almost. Once you sit back down and tell me how this little piece of...whatever it is got *made* that way and ended up in your hands, maybe I can help you figure out something else from there."

"Right." It almost felt like smiling would jinx the whole thing, including her grandmother's offer. Halsey still allowed herself a small twitch as she turned toward the armchair. This felt like the kind of win she needed right now, even if she had no idea what was going on.

"Ah-ah..." Greta pointed at the copper orb. "*After* you call back your little transmutation pet. I don't want that thing to start feeling like it's part of the décor around here."

"Fine." Halsey started toward it, but her grandmother stopped her again.

"With your magic, girl."

"What?"

"Your *non*-elemental magic." The woman's eyes glittered with anticipation. "Go ahead."

"Come on. I don't know how to—"

"Then I guess we're not having the conversation you came here for." Greta shrugged like it didn't matter to her.

She probably doesn't care whether or not we talk about it because she already knows what's going on. Or she has a theory, and as soon as I'm out of her house, that theory stays here with her. Unless I do this.

Halsey stared at the sphere and pressed her lips together. To double-check, she reached out with the magic she knew and loved to try calling the thing that way. Metal had its own life force with distinct qualities, and every type held a different variation.

When her elemental magic coursed over the copper orb, there was no response.

Guess I can't be too disappointed. I already knew it wasn't real copper. Because it wasn't real sand I pulled from that storage unit.

She had no idea what to reach for or how to call it, but she knew it had absolutely responded to her before. To what she wanted.

Great. All I want right now is for that thing to be back in my hand so Meemaw will quit playing games—

The orb shot across the room and smacked into Halsey's open palm.

"Ha!" Greta clapped once. "The proof is in the copper pudding!"

"Doesn't sound appetizing," Halsey murmured, staring at the cool, smooth sphere resting reassuringly in her hand.

"That's the thing about proof, girl. You don't have to *like* it. It simply is. Actually, that's the thing about pudding too..." The woman studied the ceiling like it would give her all the answers to everything, and Halsey made her way back into her Pappy's old armchair.

They sat silently for a moment, then Greta smacked her lips and rubbed her hands together. "So. How'd you do it?"

"I—"

"No, no. I changed my mind. Don't tell me. It's more fun that way." The woman slumped back, then immediately lurched forward and opened her mouth to say something else. After another pause, she laughed and settled against the cushions. "Start talking, girl. Forget the how and let's stick with the who, what, where, and when. And no, I didn't forget why, but I hardly think that applies in this situation. Go."

Halsey dove into the story of how the strange copper orb had come into both existence and her possession at the same time. Greta didn't interrupt, even when her granddaughter explained the difference in magic feel between the two types of sand in the silver coffin's insanely secure and now empty storage unit at the Dublin warehouse. Or when Halsey revealed that Brigham hadn't noticed that difference, even after she'd pointed it out to him.

She fully expected her grandmother to cut in at least once as she tried to describe how she pulled the leftover magical sand from someone else's spell to create the orb.

However, the older woman didn't utter a word, though her stare moved to the coffee table between them as she listened.

"After the warehouse, we waited around for a few days until Seamus finally decided it would be fun to text Brigham back, I guess." Halsey shrugged. "He was freaked out about it."

Greta snorted. "I bet."

"The weird thing is I don't think anyone else can see the thing. Regular humans, I mean. I had this thing in my hand the whole time, and nobody said a word about it. Honestly, I don't think they even saw all the extra sand in the unit."

"Hmm."

When her grandmother said nothing further, Halsey prodded, "So what is it?"

Greta stroked her chin, then dropped her hand to her lap and sighed. "Beats me."

"Really, Meemaw?"

"Hey, I still know a lot more than you. We happen to be at the same level of cluelessness on this one."

"Okay, then, how about pointing me in the right direction?"

The older woman raised an eyebrow. "If I were you, I'd ask the sand."

Halsey's shoulders slumped. "That's it?"

"It's a good start. You should seriously consider it. You should also consider how you're going to bring all this to light, which I assume you'll end up doing one way or the other. We both know how well it'll go over with the Council when they hear you and Brigham jetted off to Ireland again without so much as leaving a note."

"Ireland wasn't a mission. At least, not this second time." Halsey fixed her grandmother with a playful frown, not sure if the woman was serious about sharing with the Council or trying to give Halsey a hard time. "We didn't have to leave a note."

"They'll think you're trying to go behind their backs."

She laughed sharply. "I *am* trying to go behind their backs. Last time I tried running back to the Council to tell them something big, important, and potentially world-changing, they suspended me for a month."

Greta pursed her lips and shrugged.

"They didn't order me *not* to look into this on my own, though. So that's exactly what I'm gonna do. Until they start sending operatives out on monster missions again, it's the best use of my time."

"Ah, yes. Time. Sand. Sands of time… Isn't that a phrase somewhere?"

Wow. She's not making this an easy 'go get answers from Meemaw' chat.

Halsey leaned back in the armchair and studied the copper orb again. "I think it has something to do with an hourglass. The phrase would apply, at least."

"That's it." Greta wagged a finger. "Hourglass. That's actually quite fitting."

"Why's that?"

"Hmm? Oh. No reason."

It took all the young elemental's effort not to start shouting at the woman to get to the point already. "So after I told you everything, your only advice is to *ask the sand?*"

"And the living records, girl. Don't forget those. The two have a tendency to go hand in hand. Sometimes.

Though I personally haven't checked in many, *many* years..."

Damn it. I was so sure she could help me figure this out. Now she's into 'act crazy so no one will bother me' mode again.

Halsey was ready to pack up the sphere, give her grandmother a stiff goodbye, and look elsewhere for anything useful. Then Greta sucked in a sharp breath and met her granddaughter's gaze with a smile of realization.

"Like I said, girl, I'm willing to point you in the right direction. I'm pretty sure I know what that is, but you'll have to go check it out for yourself."

All the tension and frustration fizzled out of Halsey, and she matched Greta's beaming grin. "Deal."

CHAPTER SIX

Present time

Fifteen minutes after Halsey glimpsed a blood rune tattooed on the back of a stranger's neck, she and Brigham reached their destination at the farthest end of the Istanbul bazaar.

The Ambrosius Council had handled all the communications with their contact in Turkey, so the only information the cousins had was what they'd received during their mission briefing. Which meant they had no idea what to expect other than the fact that their contact Yusuf Burakgazi would be waiting for them somewhere in the vicinity of the cushions-and-pillows vendor stall.

They stepped into the stall, which was more like a tent with colorful cloth walls and an open entrance. Brigham leaned toward Halsey and muttered, "Would've been nice to at least get a picture of the guy first, right?"

"A name's gotta be good enough," she replied, then pulled her hands from her jacket pockets. She didn't want to be holding the copper orb once they met Burakgazi.

All I had was Aydem's name and a location, and I thought that was good enough. If I'd had a picture, too, I'd know if the guy in the dark jacket with a blood rune on his neck was the man I wanted to meet. Not sure either of those options is better at this point.

Brigham walked faster than her across the tent's interior and caught the attention of an incredibly tall, emaciated man in his mid-to-late fifties behind the folding table. Smoke from the tobacco pipe between his lips filled the tent with a pungently sweet smell. He slowly removed the pipe as Brigham approached.

This guy looks like he'd fit right in with those men at Iyi Çay.

Brigham nodded at the man, then scanned the stacked shelves packed full of cushions on either side of the table. "Hey, how ya doin'? My partner and I are meeting a Mr. Burakgazi here. Any idea where we can find him?"

The man slid the end of the pipe back between his lips, puffed a few times, then smacked his lips as he removed it again. "Name."

"Ambrosius."

The man leaned sideways to peer past Brigham at Halsey. After scrutinizing her, he turned and muttered, "Follow me."

"Thank you." Brigham looked over his shoulder at his cousin and raised his eyebrows.

Not sure what the once-over was all about, but at least we're in the right place, and the gatekeeper's willing to take us at our word. Big Guy could take a page outta this dude's book.

Halsey nodded back and followed her partner and the man with the pipe around the table toward the back wall of the tent. Which clearly wasn't a back wall as the man swept a large portion of the decorative tapestry aside and motioned for the cousins to enter first.

He didn't come with them. Instead, he let the cloth fall back behind them.

She and Brigham stood in a narrow walkway with the thick tapestry of the stall behind them and another one three feet ahead.

"Well, this is exciting," Brigham muttered as he looked around. "Has a kinda fun-house vibe, you know?"

She snorted and studied the fabric in front of them. "Sure. The kind you're not allowed to walk through unaccompanied because the guy who runs the place might be a *little* too cautious."

"Of course he's cautious, Hal. Dude's got a monster problem so bad he had to call in the professionals."

"Right, but the level of bad for *him* doesn't tell us anything useful."

"True..."

Before they could discuss any more about the mission, the tapestry was swept aside, and a man even bigger and more hulking than Big Guy from the tea shop looked the cousins over before joining them in the narrow space. The fabric dropped behind him with a thick *whump*, then he stepped in front of Brigham and spread his arms to the sides.

Brigham only stared at the guy until it dawned on him. "Seriously? We're getting frisked now?"

The man who was clearly acting as security didn't reply. When Brigham spread his arms and nodded, the silent guy grunted and efficiently patted down the first of his employer's new guests.

Brigham sniggered. "This is a first."

"First time we have to meet somebody in person to get the full details on a monster," she muttered. "First time we have to meet anybody, *period*."

The security guy paused at Brigham's hips, pointed, and nodded. Brigham sighed before lifting the hem of his loose, sweat-damp linen shirt. Doing so revealed the hip holster and pistol strapped into it, and he smiled sheepishly at Security Guy. "All part of the job, my man."

Security Guy gestured for the firearm to be handed over, and Brigham complied.

I'm guessing the only thing Burakgazi and his men know about us *is that we successfully hunt monsters and fix monster problems. Probably not that there's magic involved most of the time, or why bother disarming us first?*

After Security Guy tucked Brigham's gun under one arm and finished patting down the first Ambrosius, he nudged Brigham aside and turned toward Halsey.

"You know what?" She raised both hands and nodded at the guy. "I'll make it easy for you."

First came the long dagger sheathed at her hip, easy enough to discard by unfastening the belt that held it in place. She handed that over, then knelt to pull smaller throwing knives from first her right boot, then her left. After that, she lifted the back of her jacket to unholster the super-compact pistol she'd been carrying.

Security Guy watched her impassively as he accepted weapon after weapon. Brigham watched, too, his eyes widening when each new hiding place was revealed. "Jesus."

"What?"

"It's a meeting with a *client*, Hal. Not the actual monster."

"First actual client we've ever taken on. Who didn't give the Council nearly enough information for an accurate briefing." She was only a little surprised when Security Guy set her weapons on the ground before gesturing for her to spread her arms. So she did. "Being a little extra-prepared seemed like a good idea."

He snorted. "You call that a little?"

"Uh-huh. And you know what? Next time we actually need it, you'll thank me."

"Probably, yeah."

Don't need to tell him I'm packing all this because I had no idea what to expect from that chat with Aydem. Though Meemaw wouldn't send me to meet with someone more dangerous than the creeps and weirdos I already run into. Then again, when a dude's name and 'talk to the living records' are used in the same sentence, it's kinda hard not to think of creeps and weirdos.

The image of the man in the dark jacket entered her mind again and made things more complicated. Why was he in the tea shop? Had he been there to talk to Aydem or someone else? *Was* he Aydem? Why had he looked at her like he'd known who she was?

Come on, Halsey. Leave the secret side projects for when you're not *actively working on a mission. The only thing you need to focus on right now is this meeting.*

After Security Guy finished patting her down, he stopped beside the pile of weapons stacked neatly on the ground. He pulled aside the heavy tapestry he'd entered from behind and dipped his head as he gestured for them to enter.

Halsey forced herself not to react to a surprising piece of new information about the copper sphere.

I figured normies couldn't see the thing, but he patted down every inch of me. And...what? He couldn't feel the solid, round lump under his hand? Or did it simply not register?

She'd have to figure that out later and on her own. Maybe when she finally met with Aydem, *if* she got the chance while she and her cousin were still in Turkey. She definitely intended to make time for it.

"Thanks, man." Brigham grinned, but that only made Security Guy frown in confusion as the cousins passed into the next room.

It was strange to think about a vendor's tent having more than one "room," but here one was. The space in front of them now was covered with the same thick, heavy tapestries in traditional Turkish designs. That included the ceiling, which held several strings of golden-yellow LED lights to give the place a decorative air. Round, bulky cushions lined the back half of the room to form a square-edged U-shape of dark red, royal purple, and gold. Three low tables with cushion seating were spaced out, one for each wall.

Neither the right nor left table was occupied, though a tall, muscular, expressionless man stood in front of each with their arms folded and their feet squarely planted. They were built like Security Guy, and their gazes never left the Ambrosius cousins. Neither of them looked particularly worried about their guests, though. Beyond the sheer size of them, Halsey figured their confidence had to do with how close they stood to the man seated at the third table against the tent's far wall.

If we tried anything, they'd be on us before their boss could get to his feet. Not like we're gonna try anything anyway. It's a damn chat about a monster, not a shakedown.

The air of secrecy, high security, and prioritizing the safety of one man felt like too much for the present circumstances. Yet this was what the cousins had to work with. Even if they'd wanted to back down from this strange start to a hunting mission, they couldn't. The Council had assigned them to it with a pseudo-compliment about Halsey and Brigham being the best team for the job despite "personal opinions."

If Burakgazi has the resources to put all this together, he's probably paying us pretty well. Which, again, is super-weird because the Council can alchemize any funds it needs. Okay, though.

So they were in the presence of a Turkish man who valued his privacy as well as his safety when contracting elemental monster hunters who'd never heard of him. She couldn't have said why the thought occurred to her, but Halsey hoped Brigham didn't do or say anything to get them kicked off the job.

She shot her cousin a sidelong glance, then she jabbed an elbow in his side and hissed, "Dude, the hat."

"What?" He raised a hand toward his new kufi. "Come on. I just bought it."

"Well, if *you* don't take it off, *I* will," she whispered as they crossed the enormous tent room. "Then I'll destroy it, and you'll have to go buy another one anyway."

Her cousin looked both appalled and a little frightened

as he leaned away from her, but he grabbed the brim and slid the hat off. "Didn't know you had a thing about hats."

"I don't. Something tells me *he* might, though." It was hard to nod subtly toward the person she meant when there were only three other people in the room, and two of them were staring at her.

The third had to be Burakgazi. He didn't look at them, even when Brigham removed his hat and whisked it behind his back. Instead, the man who'd called an emergency meeting with "the best team the Ambrosius Clan had to offer" sat behind the low, round table on a mound of glittering cushions. He stared at an open magazine as he put what Halsey first thought was the end of a pipe in his mouth.

The tent filled with a hissing gurgle that sounded like a home coffeemaker reaching the end of its brew cycle. When the noise stopped, Burakgazi lifted his chin and blew out an enormous cloud of thick white vapor that obscured him from view.

Okay, so it's a hookah. The chances of Brigham embarrassing himself just went way up.

Her cousin had a similar thought as he stared at the hookah and pressed his lips together, but only because he was still interested in trying the thing at least once.

A sweet, fruity scent filtered toward them as the white cloud faded into curling tendrils that didn't completely disappear.

Then, without warning, both bodyguards stepped toward each other and met in the center to block the cousins from going any farther.

Halsey kept her face expressionless as she studied their

features. *I already paid for something I didn't get once today. Not interested in shelling out another toll before the guy I'm supposed to meet takes the money and runs. Doesn't matter that I paid Big Guy with gold from his own spoons. It's the principle of it.*

Her senses ramped to high alert as she tried to keep her cool. However, Brigham grinned at the bodyguards and rubbed his hands together. "Gentlemen." He spread his arms aside. "We already got the all-clear from the first guy back there, but I'm up for round two if you are."

The guys looked him over, then the man standing in front of Brigham reached out and pried the kufi from its owner's fingers. Brigham stuttered a groan of protest and almost reached to take it back before he remembered why they were here. The guy was most likely holding onto it for him until they were finished here.

That didn't stop him from frowning at his hat while the bodyguards returned to their places beside the empty tables. He shot Halsey one of the most heartbroken looks she'd ever seen.

It's only a hat, cuz. Monsters kinda take priority. Especially now.

Burakgazi's rich, commanding, slightly accented voice filled the tent. "My apologies for all the hoops you've had to jump through on your way here. Arranging meetings with my clients and tending to daily operations are tricky on their own already. I thought it more prudent to separate my reputation in that realm from our business together in this one. I'm sure you understand."

"Not a problem," Brigham replied, sounding like he couldn't care less about his hat being taken from him.

Halsey tried not to frown at their contact. *He doesn't want to mix his real business with his personal business? Or he thinks we'll ruin his reputation if we're seen together? Can't blame him, really. Anyone who reaches out to a private militia specializing in* monsters *would probably look like a nutjob to their friends. Or clients, in his case.*

"We're glad you reached out," Halsey added with a nod.

It was hard to make out the details of Burakgazi's facial features through the undulating threads of white hookah smoke, but she thought the man raised his eyebrows at her words before he sat back against the cushions.

"I wouldn't be too glad of anything yet. We still have quite a bit to discuss. After that, I think you two will have more than enough on your plate to keep you busy." He waved them toward the table. "Come join me, and we'll get down to it."

CHAPTER SEVEN

The Ambrosius cousins weren't stopped again as they approached their contact. After they reached the table and the hookah vapor had dissipated, Halsey fought back surprise at her first clear glimpse of Yusuf Burakgazi's face.

He couldn't have been much older than her and Brigham, probably around thirty. His hair was cut short at the sides and a little longer on top, which he'd gelled just enough to capture that messy-wet-hair look. Though he was seated on a tent floor, he was dressed for a more formal meeting. His gray business suit was as well-tailored as his crisp, off-white collared shirt, though he'd taken off the gray jacket and rolled up his shirtsleeves.

What most caught Halsey off guard were shiny, red-brown leather dress shoes next to the jacket folded on the tent floor.

Barefoot in a business suit. You don't see that in many meetings.

"Please." Burakgazi gestured toward the cushions opposite him. His smile was warm, inviting, and not what the cousins had expected based on the little information they'd received about him in their briefing.

That made it easier for them to awkwardly hunker down on the scattered mounds of pillows and cushions. It wasn't as hard as it looked to get comfortable, and Halsey rearranged the cushions beneath her before popping off her sneakers and setting them aside. She pulled her legs in close to cross them beneath herself and waited for her cousin to do the same.

Brigham had a harder time finding a comfortable position. Maybe it was because he refused to take off his shoes. Either way, Halsey and Burakgazi waited in semi-amused silence for her partner to quit fidgeting so they could officially begin their meeting.

When the squirming took longer than expected, Burakgazi frowned and released a confused chuckle. "Would you like me to fetch you a chair?"

"What? No." That was all it took to get Brigham to stop. He even clasped his hands together and rested them in his lap. "Sorry. Not used to it."

"Well, I imagine if there's anything you *are* used to, it's how to adjust to new things. Or to old things changing. Would you agree?"

Huh. Sounds like the Council told him just enough to make things interesting. Or he's fishing and got lucky with a random guess.

"I'd say that's fairly accurate," Halsey replied.

Burakgazi looked sharply at her as if he'd forgotten she was there. His smile widened, and he nodded. "I realize that was vague. Before we get into further detail, please. Remind me of your names."

Halsey narrowed her eyes. *We only gave our last name, and he knows it.*

Her cousin didn't seem suspicious of their contact's strange way of kicking off the personal introductions. Then again, when Brigham sat in a room, or a tent, with someone he was determined to know more about, he tended to act like he hadn't noticed anything. Apparently, people were more likely to be open and honest when they thought they were talking to a scatterbrain or a goofball. Or maybe it was those Brigham Ambrosius vibes. He felt more comfortable acting like he wasn't picking apart every detail of this meeting.

"My name's Brigham," he stated with a proud smile. "And this is my cousin, Halsey."

"Lovely to meet you both. You came all this way from the United States to speak with *me*. I'm both flattered and grateful."

Why does it feel like he's trying to catch us in a lie?

The second she asked herself that question, the answer came to her. "We came here to speak with Yusuf Burakgazi, yeah. At this point, we're really hoping that's you."

"Hmm. And if it's not?"

Brigham sniggered. "Well, *that'd* be embarrassing."

Halsey leaned toward the table. "We'd have to cut this conversation short. We have a job to do here, and part of it includes speaking only to Yusuf Burakgazi. Those were the terms."

This time when he smiled, it didn't feel condescending. "Then I'm sure we can all agree there's no need to waste anyone's time this afternoon." The man placed a hand over his heart and dipped his head. "Please. Call me Yusuf."

"All right." Brigham thrust a hand over the table. "Nice to meet you too, Yusuf."

Burakgazi stared at his hand for a second before accepting it for a brief, limp shake. After watching him almost refuse her cousin's gesture, Halsey didn't think it was worth it to try shaking hands herself. That decision was made easier and less awkward when Burakgazi didn't offer. In fact, he looked queasy after touching Brigham. Strange, but not enough to cause any real concern.

It's not like Brigham's a dirty guy. Some people really don't like touching other people, I guess.

The man recovered quickly from his distaste and raised the tip of the hookah hose to his lips again. He paused and looked between the cousins. "You don't mind, do you?"

Halsey shook her head.

"Go right ahead," Brigham replied. "Looks fun."

"Yes, I do enjoy it." Burakgazi took a long pull from the tip of the hose, and the hookah released another hissing burble. He tilted his head back and exhaled another massive cloud of thick white smoke.

The fact that he didn't offer to share wasn't lost on Halsey, but she didn't think even Brigham would've accepted the offer anyway.

This guy's trying to make us squirm to see what happens. Now I'm really curious what the Council told him about us.

The tent fell silent while Burakgazi dragged from the hookah again. When he finished, he hooked the hose around one of the device's extended arms, then rubbed his hands together. "So, I assume you've both been made aware of your reason for being here."

Brigham nodded. "That's why we're here."

"Indeed. Now, what did your employers tell you about my...situation?"

Brigham cleared his throat, and Halsey knew he was trying to cover a laugh.

Technically, we are *employed by the Council. I guess talking to anyone who holds a Council seat is sitting down for a business meeting. Weird to hear someone else say it out loud, though.*

"They told us you're the one who initiated contact," Brigham replied, all hint of joking or cluelessness gone. "You requested help from the Ambrosius Clan with a..." He glanced over his shoulder, but the bodyguards stood perfectly still in front of their respective empty tables, not reacting in any way. "*Unique* problem," he finished.

"Don't worry about them." Burakgazi nodded across the tent. "They don't speak English. I'd like for us to all speak freely here. A lot of things can get lost in translation when we're forced to read between the lines."

"Huh. Okay." Brigham's smile grew. "A monster problem, then."

"Chimera," Halsey chimed in. "To be specific."

The man looked back and forth between them. "Neither of you seems particularly surprised or disheartened by that."

"Well, it's not the first monster we've been sent out to take care of."

"Not even our first chimera," Brigham added. "I know it's probably weird to hear strangers talking about this stuff like it's an everyday thing, but for us, it is. This is what we do. Which you already knew, because you came to the Ambrosius Clan so we could deal with this thing for you."

Halsey folded her hands in her lap and nodded. "So if

we don't look surprised or disheartened, it's because we're not."

For their first sit-down with a "client" who clearly needed convincing of their skills and qualifications as much as he needed outside help, Halsey was proud of the way they'd tag-teamed their statements. Calm. Confident. Reassuring. That was how they felt about the mission despite the fact that right now, it seemed more like an interview.

She expected Burakgazi to take them at their word that they could handle his chimera problem, so all they'd need was the when and where.

Instead, the man lifted the hookah hose to his lips again. "You're not concerned in the slightest?"

Brigham eyed the end of the hose but still didn't ask to try it. "Not even a little, Yusuf."

"Well, you should be." Burakgazi inhaled through the hookah hose, watching for a reaction while the smoking device hissed and bubbled.

Halsey stared back at him and hoped her cousin was doing the same. *This guy's blowing smoke. In more ways than one. If this was coming from another elemental, maybe I'd be concerned, but he's a normie. Granted, he knows about monsters and that the Ambrosia Clan militia exists, but that's not enough to make him an expert on doing* our *jobs.*

The cousins waited as their new client helped himself to a few more puffs.

Halsey clenched her hands in her lap under the edge of the table and kept her mouth shut until the man was ready to keep talking.

This is exactly why we don't do clients. Monsters are easy.

They don't make you wait, they don't screw with your head before going in for a job, and they don't keep secrets. Not that I know of, anyway.

"Mind telling us why that is?" Brigham prompted with a crooked smile. To anyone who didn't know him, he looked like he didn't have a care in the world. His partner knew differently.

Burakgazi gazed at the hose in his hand, then returned a similar smile that set off multiple warning alarms in Halsey's mind. "That's why we're all here, isn't it?"

There's something off about this guy. I can't start accusing him of "being a little suspicious" when everything about this meeting and this entire mission is suspicious.

When their cautious host didn't say anything else, she couldn't help but feel they'd missed an important piece of the puzzle. "Yusuf, how exactly did you hear about us?"

The man's closed-lipped smile widened. "I'm sorry?"

"It's not like we have a website or any active advertising." She shrugged and decided to ignore Brigham's baffled expression. "So, before we do anything else, I'd like to hear how you knew to contact the Ambrosius Clan."

Burakgazi drew a deep breath and held her gaze. Though he kept smiling, Halsey sensed something not so friendly beneath that smile.

Maybe he doesn't like being questioned. It probably doesn't happen much.

The man blinked, dropped his gaze, and chuckled. "Word of mouth is a valuable commodity in certain circles. I asked around for the best in this…particular industry, and in response, I received the contact information for your organization."

"Interesting," Brigham muttered.

"Yes, it is." Halsey tilted her head and fixed their contact with a look she'd seen many times before from her Uncle Arthur, from the other Council members, from her own father. A deeper understanding of *why* they'd given her that look almost made her grimace. "Because we generally don't take requests. Or contracts."

"And I generally don't come across a troublesome situation I can't handle on my own," he replied flatly. "Yes, that does include supernatural phenomena."

So he's seen monsters before. In a fleeting moment of brazen curiosity, Halsey reached out with her magic to scan the man. Like every other bit of matter in the natural world, humans had their own types of life energy with different energetic patterns. Elementals and normies felt especially different from each other because one type had magic, and the other didn't.

Yusuf Burakgazi did not.

As soon as she knew for certain, she almost sighed in relief. At the same moment, Burakgazi narrowed his eyes and paused as if he'd sensed she was attempting something but couldn't put his finger on what.

And if he'd had magic? Well, I guess both our covers would've been blown. At least I'd know if he was hiding something other than the fact that he's meeting with two bona fide monster hunters in a private tent in a crowded Turkish bazaar.

Halsey raised her chin and played it off like she hadn't secretly scanned him for magic. "Who told you about us?"

The corner of the man's mouth twitched, and his smile faded. "I'm not at liberty to discuss anyone else's identity or affairs but my own."

"Fair enough," Brigham muttered and nodded curtly. "So let's—"

"I'm sorry, Yusuf," Halsey interrupted. "We *are* at liberty to decline any request for our services if we feel the information we've received isn't sufficient or complete enough to successfully do our job. I'm starting to feel like we're heading in that direction."

The tense silence seemed more awkward when Halsey realized she could no longer feel her cousin's stare. It was easy to imagine him muttering under his breath, *"Hal, what the hell are you doing?"* Fortunately, he let her keep the lead and didn't say a word.

Finally, Burakgazi leaned back against the cushions behind him. "I was under the impression that you two are soldiers."

"Not the kind you're thinking of."

"But soldiers nonetheless." He raised his eyebrows. "I understand a soldier's job is to carry out their orders. Without question."

Brigham cleared his throat. "Well, that's technically true—"

"But we're a private organization," Halsey continued because it was clear her cousin was close to rolling over for this guy. That wasn't helping. "The rules for *our organization* are a little different than anything else you've heard of before. You contacted the Ambrosius Council and requested the best team to get the job done for you. They sent us."

"Apparently, they failed to notify me that I would be questioned indiscriminately because of it. Perhaps this was a mistake."

CHAPTER EIGHT

This guy won't give up.

Halsey paused, not quite sure how to handle their only contact combatting her at every turn. Talking about monsters and the exchange of information wasn't part of the process for any of her past missions, and their militia training didn't include negotiating with normies who might know about magic in addition to monsters.

She had no idea what to do.

Brigham was her mission partner for a good reason. Whether or not he agreed with her going against the plan, he wouldn't hang her out to dry. Apparently, it had taken him a bit longer to pick up on her intentions than usual. Now, he backed her up completely. Like he always did.

"Respectfully, Yusuf," he began with a smile. "You requested the use of our services and expertise without offering any information beyond when and where to meet. *We* were under the impression you would be forthcoming with the rest of those details once we met with you in person. This is what my partner's asking for."

The man clicked his tongue. "That wasn't included in my arrangement with your superiors."

"It wasn't specifically excluded, either." Brigham spread his arms and shrugged. "We have our orders, yes. On a broad scale, those orders were to meet with you, gather the necessary information to *fully* assess the situation, and take care of this little problem for you. Those parameters are fairly broad, and they were left that way for a good reason."

Burakgazi inhaled deeply through his nose as he studied them. It was a small, wordless concession on his part, and Halsey smiled. They'd gotten him where he needed to be, so they could do what they needed to do.

"The second our boots left the ground in the U.S., the full authority to assess this specific situation was placed in our hands. Including whether or not to move forward in offering our services within reasonable means." Halsey continued confidently. "The operative word here is *reasonable*, Yusuf. There's no Ambrosius Clan base in Turkey. We don't have additional access to a network or resources anywhere in the Mediterranean or surrounding areas. We're out here on our own, answering *your* request. Whether we continue moving forward with this mission is at *our* sole discretion."

"Are we soldiers?" Brigham bobbed his head in mock consideration. "In a way, sure. You've also made us private contractors, and if we feel like the mission is already compromised before we've even gotten started, we can walk away."

All traces of amusement disappeared from Burakgazi's face. Surprise, tinged with irritation, replaced it. When he let out a long, noisy sigh through his nose, it seemed he'd realized he wasn't getting what he wanted unless he gave them what *they* wanted first. He finally muttered, "This wasn't at all what I expected."

"Looks like we're on the same page, then," Halsey replied. Beside her, Brigham broke into a beaming grin.

If he doesn't start talking in the next ten seconds, I guess we're done here. And if he reaches for that stupid hose one more time, I'm throwing the whole damn thing across this tent before we call it a day.

It almost felt like the mission was heading in that direction already as they sat around the table in expectant silence.

Neither of the cousins expected Burakgazi to lurch out of his own stillness, throw his head back, and roar with laughter.

Halsey and Brigham exchanged confused, slightly worried looks.

Or the Council sent us out here to talk to a madman, and we officially broke him.

Burakgazi gasped for breath between gales of laughter, then slapped his hands together before shaking a finger at them. "Excellent. That was superb!"

Brigham chuckled. "Glad you think so."

"You two—" The man laughed again and shook his head. "You two are everything your superiors said you were and much more. Honestly, I think they underestimate you. Or at least, they undersold your thoroughness."

Great. So the Council told this guy they were sending their best, and he still *thought we wouldn't be good enough. Why am I not surprised?*

Halsey kept a straight face despite their contact's

continuous chuckling as he ran a hand over the top of his dark, gelled hair. "I take it this means you approve of their choice."

"Now? Absolutely."

Brigham snorted and folded his arms. "So all that was a test."

"Of course it was." Burakgazi opened his arms and grinned. "When you're operating in a world of secrets more terrifying and impossible than the majority of this planet's population can even *begin* to fathom, there's no such thing as being too careful. Don't get me wrong. Your organization came highly recommended. By necessity, though, I'm in the habit of assessing qualifications for myself."

"We haven't given you our qualifications," Halsey muttered.

"The kind I'm looking for, Miss Ambrosius? Yes. You most certainly did." The man fixed her with a knowing smile. "As you're both aware, this is very sensitive information. I couldn't deliver it into the hands of any private contractor saying they're adept at this sort of thing. These days, people say whatever they think you want to hear. Especially with half a million on the line."

Brigham forced a cough before pressing a fist to his mouth.

No shit. The Council would rather send us all the way out here for an easy half-million than turn it down. Alchemizing half a million in gold is a hell of a lot of man-hours, anyway.

Burakgazi continued jovially. "To be clear, your experience and qualifications in the field were never in question. However, I am somewhat in the business of assessing a person's character and business conduct. Or that of a team, in this case. I refuse to work with anyone who can't think for themselves."

Halsey chortled. "Well, no one ever said we don't do that."

Brigham tried to cover a laugh with another forced cough.

"Indeed." Burakgazi held Halsey's gaze, which gave her the distinct feeling he knew what she was thinking.

He doesn't have magic, so there's no chance he could've picked up on what I'm thinking. Still, this guy knows way more than he's letting on.

Their contact sighed in contentment and nodded. "With something like this, it's especially crucial those I *do* choose to work with possess a certain level of…discernment. In any and all affairs. Clearly, neither of you is willing to enter into an agreement with a stranger who fails to provide any relevant information, though you *were* willing to come all this way in an attempt to glean that information for yourselves. And you didn't give an inch."

"Yep." Brigham flashed another grin but looked like he was about to either crack up laughing or leap off the cushions and bolt from the tent. "That *is* something our superiors would say about us."

"Well, I can assure you that your point of contact didn't imply that was the case. I had a feeling it would be, though. Call it hopeful optimism. So far, the two of you have exceeded my expectations."

"Huh." Halsey tilted her head, still unsure what to think of the wealthy, well-educated, business-forward Turk who spoke like he was at least twice their age instead of only a few years older. "Doesn't sound like you set the bar very high."

"When you've finalized as many deals in any number of industries as I have, Miss Ambrosius, a baseline of low expectations is necessary. Which is why I'm looking forward to working with the two of you. Toward mutual benefit, of course."

"Oh, sure." Brigham nodded sagely like they got paid half a million dollars to go after a single monster every day. "Mutual benefit."

We have no idea how much of that "fee" is going into our pockets, if any. The Council failed to mention that part. Again.

"So." Halsey raised an eyebrow. "Does that mean you'll answer our questions?"

"I wouldn't have it any other way, Miss Ambrosius. You've already answered mine."

Being called *Miss Ambrosius* made her want to correct him, call off the whole thing, or both. Even the Ambrosius estate house staff stuck to the casual *Miss Halsey*, though plenty of them simply called her Hal in passing or when there was no one else around. It took a lot of effort not to grimace at the moniker now, and the man had used it at least three times already.

That's not why we're here. Something tells me Mr. Burakgazi doesn't like being corrected after *he's done his little tests.*

"Great." She nodded and didn't bother trying to smile because she also had the feeling this guy could tell when an expression wasn't genuine. Plus, this was business. They didn't need the man to like them any more than he already did. "So let's start with where you heard about us."

"We will. Absolutely. First, I think it's only fitting we

celebrate this new and promising partnership. As a token of my gratitude, of course. I'm rarely impressed."

Yeah, and I bet he's rarely humble about it, either.

Halsey did force a smile then. It was the next best thing to scowling. "I think we—"

"To new and promising partnerships," Brigham interrupted without hesitation or wariness. "Thank you."

Burakgazi looked thoroughly pleased by the response but shook his head and waved off the comment. "It's the least I can do. Ensar?"

The guard who *wasn't* holding Brigham's hat like a human coat rack turned toward his boss and clasped his hands in front. Burakgazi said something in rapid Turkish.

Ensar nodded curtly and marched from the tent to carry out whatever instructions he'd been given, and Burakgazi sat back against his cushions again. This time, he propped an elbow on one of the stacks and looked every inch a king reclining on his throne. "When did you get in?"

"To Turkey?" Brigham shot his cousin a glance, and Halsey dipped her head to signal for him to continue. This part was *his* specialty. Small talk and congenial conversation while wheedling out the information they needed. "Our flight got in just after six this morning."

"Ah. Good." Burakgazi looked pleased by that. "Then may I safely assume you haven't yet had the time to sit down for a proper meal?"

Brigham's face lit up at the prospect of food, which would have happened even if the cousins had eaten right before stepping from their rental car to head into the bazaar. "You may."

"Excellent." The man reached for the end of his hookah

hose, unwound it from its hook, and drew in through the tip.

Brigham gazed at the smoking device with a renewed sense of hopeful excitement and interest, and Halsey laughed inwardly.

Well, at least this could've gone a whole lot worse. Not sure how I feel about my partner and the militia's first client being BFFs, but hey. Never hurts to have friends in high places.

Clearly, Yusuf Burakgazi belonged to several exclusive circles both in business and Turkish society. The only problem was that Halsey had no idea where those "high places" were or what kind of people they contained.

If the Council wants this to be a repeat thing, they need to fold business relations into our militia training.

CHAPTER NINE

After learning they'd be sharing a meal with their mission contact, Halsey expected a long wait. They were sitting in a private tent at the back of a bazaar and not in a fast-paced restaurant. The thought of all the time they'd waste in here while only one bodyguard stood stiffly at attention with Brigham's hat, and Yusuf filled the tent with nauseatingly sweet hookah vapor made her want to scream.

Halsey Ambrosius excelled at taking action and quickly resolving issues, whatever they happened to be. This wasn't included in her skillset.

On the other hand, Brigham thrived in this kind of scenario. It didn't matter that this was the first time the Ambrosius Council had assigned a mission requiring diplomacy or any kind of human interaction. Her cousin had been born with the gift of gab. Until now, he'd only used it for Council meetings, potentially volatile mission debriefings, and any time he wanted something from someone.

As far as Halsey knew, the only person it didn't work on was herself.

"That's because you're a brute," he used to tell her after they'd graduated from their militia training. "You'd rather run to the range, blow up a mountain, or throw those stupid axes at a dead tree than sit down and *talk* to somebody."

"I'd rather throw those axes at your face right now," she'd replied, and they both cracked up laughing before moving on to something else.

Now, she was grateful for the stark differences between them. Those differences were part of what had always made them a good team. Trying to imagine what this meeting would have looked like *without* Brigham, or with a different partner like Owen The Burger or even Rupert, was almost physically painful.

So while they waited for Ensar to bring whatever their paying client considered "a proper meal," Brigham kept Burakgazi engaged in conversation about absolutely nothing. And Halsey had an opportunity to further size up the man who'd requested their presence but still hadn't told them anything useful.

Except for that little quip about how worried he thinks we should be. The most we've established there is that he's seen monsters before and usually doesn't need help, but one little chimera is too much for him.

She managed to drown out the conversation between Brigham and Burakgazi so she could narrow in on what they knew about the man.

On a surface level? He's wealthy. Maybe Turkish nobility or close to it, if that's even a thing. His name didn't come up on any public records, so either he's using a pseudonym, or he's good at keeping himself off the radar. Probably because he holds meetings in private bazaar tents where no one would think to look for him.

That almost made her laugh. She cleared her throat instead, but neither Brigham nor Burakgazi seemed to notice. In fact, they kept gabbing along, laughing and nodding, filling the time and each other's heads with whatever they found so entertaining. Halsey felt almost entirely forgotten. Or invisible.

Which would be even more to our benefit right now, but I'll take what I can get.

It was impossible to tell exactly what kind of business Burakgazi normally conducted, even after he'd hinted at various deals and associations in multiple industries. Obviously, he did well for himself, or the details of *this* meeting would have been a lot different.

Her gaze fell on the man's fingers, delicately curled around the end of the hookah hose as he took drag after gurgling drag.

His nails were cut short but not manicured as she'd expect from someone who clearly cared about his appearance and reputation. Some of the ends were jagged, nowhere near evenly filed. He'd obviously tried to repair the damage with some kind of ointment or lotion that made the nailbeds look slightly oily, but he hadn't managed to hide the redness or the bits of dry, dead skin around them.

Every time he raised the hookah hose to his lips, he held it between his thumb and the first two fingers, releasing the last two from the wooden tip. It seemed the equivalent of raising a pinky while sipping from a teacup, which would have made her laugh if she hadn't been scrutinizing the guy for clues about who he was and what he did.

She moved her focus to his palm the next time he lifted his fingers while he smoked and noticed an interesting detail. Both the heel and the top pad of his palm were coated in thick, rough-looking calluses.

So he's not the kind of boss who sits back and orders his grunts to take care of his dirty work. That might be a plus.

Burakgazi finished inhaling another lungful of nicotine-laced strawberry flavor. As he exhaled vapor, Halsey sought something else to focus on so she wouldn't look like she was mean-mugging the guy. Which she might have been. Something about him didn't sit right with her.

She didn't trust him. He hadn't told them anything they needed to know, and he most likely wouldn't until after they broke bread together. After that, when he answered her questions like he'd promised and they had the necessary details for completing this mission?

No, she didn't think she'd trust him any more than she did now. At least she and Brigham would be able to leave the tent and discuss it privately, though.

What am I looking for while we're here? Why does this guy rub me the wrong way? It's not like I don't have experience dealing with people who think way too much of themselves and like to wave around a carrot on a stick. He doesn't have magic. Can't be planning an ambush with only one bodyguard while he's sprawled on his cushy pillow-throne. Plus, he hasn't said anything downright insulting. So far...

The lilting background drone of Brigham's voice as he told some witty, heavily detailed anecdote added to her focus. Halsey couldn't be sure what expression had settled on her face, but when Burakgazi raised the hookah hose again, her gaze was pulled back toward his hand.

Where she found one more interesting little detail.

About an inch below the heel of his palm was a patch of slightly raised scar tissue. It was the same ochre tone as the rest of Burakgazi's skin, though not nearly as tanned by the Mediterranean sun. It wasn't red or inflamed, either, meaning it wasn't a new scar.

It caught and held Halsey's attention because of its size and shape.

The scar spread between two and three inches up his wrist and into his forearm, but it didn't slash across his wrist or pucker at the ends like scars tended to do when they formed accidentally or from injury. As far as she could see, there were no other scars on his arm or hand, leaving this one a lot easier to spot.

If she'd seen this scar a few days ago, or even this morning, she probably would've written it off as an amateur attempt at tattoo removal or maybe some kind of brand. The design itself wasn't all that visible, though it clearly had been designed.

Normally, she couldn't have cared less about what other people did or didn't do to their bodies. It was none of her business.

Yet less than an hour before, she'd seen a man in a dark jacket walk out of the tea shop where she'd tried to meet with Aydem. *That* man had a crimson design tattooed on the back of his neck.

A design that looked a hell of a lot like the scar tissue on the inside of Yusuf Burakgazi's arm.

You can't know that for sure, Halsey. Jacket Man was too far away to see anything other than red and something that could have been a blood rune. This guy's sitting in front of you, and it's still not close enough to tell what that mark is. You're drawing threads together that probably have nothing to do with each other.

It was easy to tell herself these things. So much of her training and experience as a monster hunter was based on *not* jumping to conclusions. Rather, she was trained to use the knowledge she had to make educated guesses about her targets and, if necessary, pivot accordingly. However, her targets were monsters. Burakgazi was not.

She was pretty far out of her depth when it came to reading *people,* or at least reading normies. That didn't make her instincts obsolete, even in a situation like this. If her gut told her there was some kind of connection between Jacket Man and Burakgazi, there was a good chance it was right.

It usually was.

A jolt of awareness shot through her when Brigham and Burakgazi both laughed at the end of whatever story her cousin had been telling. She couldn't stop staring at the man's wrist.

I wouldn't have even seen that if we'd met him somewhere else. He's comfortable here with his shoes and suit jacket on the floor, and his sleeves rolled up. Looks like the super-careful businessman forgot about keeping one thing secret. Or maybe he was betting that we'd stop noticing things once we passed his little test.

She swallowed thickly and forced her gaze away from

his arm as the hookah stopped burbling and the man exhaled again.

Then again, may he wants us to see something. Maybe he's counting on it. If I had anything to do with blood magic and rune tattoos, I'd want someone who knew about it to say something. Wouldn't that make the perfect trap for a couple of elementals far from home?

"Right, Hal?" Brigham elbowed her and chuckled. "You remember that one."

She smiled crookedly without thinking and nodded. "How could I forget?"

"Yeah, you're telling me." Brigham returned his attention to their host and grinned again. "Point is, we've gotten used to that kinda thing over the last few years. Guess I could've made a long story a hell of a lot shorter, huh?"

Burakgazi chuckled and shook his head. "I enjoy the long version, personally. There's no character otherwise. No *flavor* to a story. And there is no denying when a story is truly a good one."

Brigham dipped his head in mock humility.

Burakgazi focused on Halsey. "Wouldn't you agree?"

She stared back at him. "I think any good story needs three things. Believability from the start, or your audience loses interest, and you might as well give up. Then you need high stakes. The kind that really socks you in the guts, you know? Toss in stakes that anyone could imagine applying to *them*, and they're invested."

Beside her, Brigham inhaled through his nose and didn't say a thing.

Burakgazi didn't once break her gaze, though he played

the part well when he released an uncertain chuckle and leaned forward. "And the third?"

"Hmm?"

"You said every good story needs three things. You've only mentioned two."

"Oh, right. Number three…" She tipped her head back to pretend she was searching for her final answer and paused long enough to feel Brigham stiffen beside her. Then she flicked her gaze toward Burakgazi's eager face and spoke the rest with a deadpan expression. "You gotta have an ending no one *ever* sees coming."

At first, the man's only reaction was to raise his eyebrows. Then his eyes narrowed. "I would *love* to hear one of *your* stories."

"I don't think so." Halsey pressed her lips together and broke his gaze, pretending to study the intricate designs woven into the tapestries that made up the walls of the tent.

"Oh, come on," Burakgazi pressed, his voice pinched into a joking whine. "The way you set up those parameters, I imagine your stories are even more riveting than your assessment. There's no need to be coy."

It sounded like Brigham choked on a breath before he cleared his throat. "She's not being coy, man. Trust me. Stories aren't her thing."

"So what *is* your thing?" the man pressed. Halsey felt his gaze roaming her despite the fact that she hadn't looked at him again.

I thought we were past the whole interrogation bit. What else does he want?

A small, quiet alarm was going off in the back of her

mind, telling her not to push her luck with this guy. She wasn't sure about the mark on his wrist, who he was, or what he did. Plus, whether he actually had any affiliation with Jacket Man, blood runes, or anything related to blood magic and the sect of humans who wielded it.

Until two months ago, the Ambrosius Clan had assumed the descendants of the Blood Matriarch were extinct. Wiped off the face of the Earth in the great war. Then Halsey had delivered six severed ogre hands with crimson blood runes etched on the palms.

That quiet alarm wasn't enough to keep her from reacting the way she usually did when she got angry, creeped out, or both.

Halsey met Burakgazi's gaze again and smirked. "My thing? Generally, I'd say it's raising the stakes and doing what most people never see coming. You know, finishing what I started."

"Ah." The man's smile widened into an open-mouthed leer, almost like he was laughing without sound. He wasn't laughing, though.

If he keeps looking at me like that, we're gonna have a serious problem.

Brigham sighed and jumped back into his friendly, conversational persona. "In other words, my partner's more action-oriented. Simple as that."

"That doesn't sound simple," Burakgazi crooned.

"Well, it's not." Brigham's smile widened as he picked up on the negative and potentially explosive effect their host's stare was having on his cousin. "As a summary, it's pretty damn accurate."

"I see." The man finally pulled his gaze away from

Halsey and went back into his easygoing, "let's enjoy ourselves now that we're all on the same page" energy. Which was how he'd spent the whole time talking to Brigham before drawing Halsey into one hell of a weird conversation topic. "So *she's* the one who does all the physical work, the actual *monster*-hunting, and you're more of her...chronicler?"

Despite the eerie tension two seconds before, Halsey couldn't control her snorting laugh at Burakgazi's inaccurate assessment.

Brigham shot her a scathing glare. "Uh...it's not *that*, either. We're partners. I know all the historical fiction and period TV shows or whatever depict the one hero going out to slay the monster while his fun little sidekick follows him around to write songs about him. It's different in real life, though. At least in *this* century."

"Well, then." Burakgazi smirked as he picked up the hookah hose again. "Clearly, I stand corrected."

The Ambrosius cousins might have corrected him on any number of additional misconceptions once they recovered from the unnerving tension in the air.

There's no way I'm not getting a Brigham-lecture after this meeting's over. I might even let him finish before I tell him about that scar.

Fortunately for all three of them, Ensar chose that moment to complete the task his employer had given him.

Halsey almost called it quits when the bodyguard threw the tapestry flap open and marched across the tent empty-handed. If Brigham wasn't on the verge of a meltdown after waiting this long for food, he would be soon.

Then the fabric drew aside once more, and two shorter

men in crisply starched white uniforms rolled a silver cart into the tent. Silver serving dishes packed the top tray, and from the way the thing wobbled across the ground, even more platters and dishes likely hid on the lower shelves behind the draped white linens.

The scents of cooked meats, flaky crusts, and strong spices filled the tent, overwhelming the cloying sweetness of Burakgazi's hookah smoke until it was nothing but a bad memory.

Another secretive, self-confident smirk passed across their host's features as he slid the smoking device toward the far side of the table. "I've been looking forward to this. There's a bit of everything here, so do feel free to try as much as you like."

"Sounds like a plan." Brigham rubbed his hands vigorously and turned to watch the men lift platters and approach to set them out on the table. Adding to the lavish feeling of the meal were these men who looked like they'd stepped from a five-star kitchen to serve it.

Burakgazi acted as if this extravagance was nothing special, which made Halsey think the cushion tent wasn't the only spot he owned at the bazaar.

One of the bodyguards removed the hookah from the table, and not another word was spoken until all the platters were laid out on the round table, along with silverware, napkins, and crystal water goblets. Still more remained on the cart, and Halsey assumed it would stay there until they finished the first few courses laid out in front of them.

The wide-eyed, ecstatic anticipation on her cousin's face said that wouldn't take long.

Even though she was pretty sure she'd lost her appetite.

Eat first, talk later. He promised he'd answer your questions, so don't blow this whole thing by being a jerk.

For the duration of their meal, Halsey's focus refused to remain on the spread of spiced and flavorful Mediterranean food. Instead, she constantly forced herself not to stare at Yusuf Burakgazi's left wrist.

CHAPTER TEN

Expecting Brigham Ambrosius to remain silent during the course of *any* meal was like expecting Halsey to carry out every order and complete every assigned mission without once questioning the Council's motives behind it. Which meant it didn't happen.

The food was incredible, though. It was easier for Halsey to focus on how much she enjoyed the food and how hungry she'd actually been rather than any other troubling thing Burakgazi might have said or done. Fortunately, she wasn't asked any other direct questions while they ate, which meant Brigham kept the peace and the casual conversation without drawing attention to the fact that his cousin didn't trust *anyone*, period.

Mostly, he and Burakgazi talked about the food, and that was fine with her. Provided after lunch, they stopped blabbering and got down to the real business.

For Halsey and Brigham Ambrosius, that business was hunting monsters. Nothing more, nothing less.

For Yusuf Burakgazi, that business contained several

different things, and the cousins were only privy to a small sliver of them today.

Halsey guessed that represented a good deal of her hesitation about the man. It was hard to pin somebody down when they were being pulled in so many different directions. That tended to make a person seem as scattered as their priorities.

However, Burakgazi continued with their meal and the ensuing conversation as if sitting down with monster hunters was all he ever did, day in and day out. The man gave the Ambrosius cousins his full attention. Now that there was food involved, he'd apparently given up on trying to pick Halsey apart to see what made her tick.

That part was definitely a relief.

Once they'd eaten everything and Brigham looked ready to start licking the platters clean, the uniformed men returned to clear the table. Then, they laid out a new course of food from the meal cart. Halsey had no idea what any of it was, but it smelled amazing. Savory and sweet at the same time. She started to rethink her previous conviction that she couldn't eat another bite.

If he keeps piling on the food to avoid the only conversation that matters, somebody's gotta put a stop to it. And it won't be Brigham.

Burakgazi smiled and nodded at his employees, looking as proud as if he'd cooked everything himself. That pride only grew when one of the men set an incredibly tall, frosted, light blue glass container in the center of the table, followed by three small glasses that looked like miniature versions of Iyi Çay's tea cups.

"A meal isn't complete without dessert." The man

gestured toward the newly laid plates. "Which we have plenty of here. Baklava, almond cookies, and *kunefe*. They can be an acquired taste if you're not accustomed to them, so don't worry about insulting me if you find yourselves not quite enjoying it."

Brigham chuckled and reached for the closest platter to serve himself some almond cookies. "That's not something you need to worry about."

Burakgazi grabbed the tall blue glass that looked like a centerpiece vase and poured something into Halsey's tea cup. "Nor is any business meeting, proposal, or agreement truly official without a drink," he added.

"Of course not," she murmured with a healthy dose of sarcasm.

The man chuckled before setting the delicate glass in front of her, now filled with a golden liquid slightly darker than white wine.

"I'm glad you agree." Burakgazi filled Brigham's glass next, smiling like they were all best friends. For the purposes of their mission, maybe they were. They still hadn't actually held that conversation yet, and Halsey was getting impatient. "This is *raki*. A traditional Turkish brandy, very much like *ouzo*. It's something of a personal tradition for me. I only share this with people I trust to fulfill their end of our arrangements, as I shall fulfill mine when it's all said and done. I hope you don't mind the flavor of anise."

After swallowing his mouthful of almond cookies and wiping the crumbs from his mouth, Brigham picked up his tiny glass of *raki* and sniffed. "Not that I know of. Licorice brandy, huh?"

"Yes. So now, we'll toast to officially mark the end of our meal together and the beginning of everything you wanted to know about this job."

"I feel like we already landed on the perfect toast." Brigham shot his cousin a warning look before subtly nodding toward the drink she hadn't touched yet.

Halsey wanted to roll her eyes, but she snatched her glass and gave it a careful whiff. It definitely smelled like anise. And ridiculously strong booze. "Remind me what that was again."

"To new and promising partnerships," Burakgazi replied as he raised his tiny glass. "I like that one."

"To new and promising partnerships," Brigham echoed, somehow making it sound natural and off-the-cuff despite having said it already before their meal.

Both men gazed at Halsey, waiting for her to do her part.

Yeah, I'm not playing copycat for a toast with a guy who assumes we have a partnership before he tells us a damn thing.

Yet being the center of attention meant she had to do *something*, so she lifted her glass and murmured, "Ditto."

Brigham pressed his lips together, Burakgazi chuckled, and the three of them sipped the *raki* together.

Halsey's fought not to smack her lips afterward in case it gave their host the wrong idea. Adding booze to the meeting was probably supposed to be a fun, friendly way to loosen them up, so everyone felt good about their new arrangement. Still, Halsey wasn't willing to let it go any further without steering the focus in a productive direction.

"The food was wonderful, Yusuf. Thank you."

Burakgazi blinked and stared at her in mute surprise as she set down her glass before folding her hands on the table. Then he laughed and cleared his throat. "You're very welcome."

Yeah, I can use my manners when I want something.

She kept smiling and felt her cousin's gaze on her as Brigham slowly sipped the *raki*. "Now that we've made our toast, I think it's time to talk business," she insisted.

"Of course." The man swallowed some of the Turkish liqueur, then brought the small glass with him when he leaned against the cushions. "You want more details about the job."

"I want more details about *you*, actually. Call it a preliminary assessment, if that's easier."

Brigham picked at the dessert trays, the only one who'd even touched the final round of food. He pretended not to notice the biting sting in his cousin's words. That included not trying to stop her from doing *her* thing now that the pleasantries and promises were out of the way.

Burakgazi didn't seem to have an opinion one way or the other. In fact, he looked focused on his drink. "Fire away."

Ooh, buddy. Don't tempt me.

Halsey maintained what she hoped was an unreadable expression. Determination mixed with amusement and a sprinkle of irritation. It was how she felt right now, which made sense, given what she knew. To their host, it was likely a confusing combination of expressions without any real explanation.

That was how she wanted to keep him. On his toes.

"Before we got into all this, I asked you how you heard about us."

"I remember."

"I'd like you to answer that first, if it's all the same to you."

The man's smile grew faker and more bitter by the second. He sucked in a sharp breath and sat up straighter, though he didn't draw himself closer to the table. "As I've already mentioned, Miss Ambrosius, my business dealings stretch across a wide range of industries. Most of them are nestled within the realm of reality-based logic and humankind's historical understanding of the world. Of course, that's operating under the assumption there *isn't* more than one reality on which to base such understanding."

"We're not the first people you've done business with who know about monsters," she replied flatly. "Good to know."

"Yes, well. I'm already fairly well-connected within this other…*secret* reality, if you will. With which the two of you and your organization are quite familiar, obviously. So when I decided I needed assistance with—"

"I want a name, Yusuf." Halsey shook her head. "Not an excuse."

She could practically hear Brigham's voice in her mind telling her to cool her jets before they blew their chances on half a million bones. Not to mention before they officially started this mission with all the necessary information. She told her cousin's imaginary voice to shut it because she'd been silent and patient all day. Now it was her turn to get to the point.

Fortunately, the real Brigham didn't try to intervene on behalf of their host's ego and their prospects of moving on to the next phase. He did knock back the rest of his *raki* in one gulp and set the empty glass on the table.

Burakgazi surprised her with his reaction. Instead of taking offense at being interrupted, the man chuckled and fixed her with the smile of a preschool teacher aimed at kids who would've shredded their own parents' last nerve.

The same look Halsey frequently received from her own family members, most of them with active seats on the Council.

That was almost worse than an offended outburst, but she had to let it slide.

"Direct and to the point." He raised his glass toward her, sipped his drink, then nodded. "You did say you were more action-oriented, and I now realize I didn't quite understand the full extent of that truth."

She only had to raise her eyebrows to reinforce that she wouldn't keep beating around the bush with this.

He could no longer look her in the eye after he gave in to her request. Burakgazi turned his dark-eyed gaze to the mound of cushions beside him, from which he pulled invisible lint. "His name is Halil Aydem."

Halsey's full stomach tried to leap into her throat, failed, and flopped back down with an accompanying wave of nausea. A flush of heat rose through her cheeks and into the top of her head.

You've gotta be kidding me.

She stared at their host, but no immediate response came to mind. All her effort had suddenly gone into maintaining her poker face.

Brigham gave her another second, then figured she probably wanted him to push their contact. He nodded like he understood everything and asked, "And who's Halil Aydem?"

"He belongs to yet another old, secretive organization dedicated to the preservation, and in some rare cases the *dissemination*, of historical records involving supernatural phenomena. Monsters, ghosts, creatures, events, timelines, family trees. You name it, this organization has something on it. And yes, that's from a number of different sources within my personal network, none of them connected to each other, and all of them quite reputable. Don't ask me if I've happened to verify these facts."

"Wouldn't dream of it," Brigham murmured with a slow nod. "What's the name of this organization Aydem belongs to?"

Burakgazi came closer to rolling his eyes than he'd been since the cousins had stepped into his private tent. The man somehow turned his petulant response into another sophisticated, albeit slightly irritated, expression. "They call themselves the Order of Skrár. From what I hear. My communication with Aydem didn't extend far enough to confirm or deny the accuracy of the name, but again, I trust my sources."

Order of Skrár. Why does that sound so damn familiar?

Brigham hummed thoughtfully and drummed his fingers on his thigh. "Records."

"Living records," Halsey muttered without realizing she'd said it out loud.

"Yes, actually." Burakgazi fixed her with a confused smile. "That's exactly right. How did you know?"

She couldn't think of any version of the truth that wasn't inappropriately personal or that wouldn't sound like an insane, boldfaced lie. Instead, she grabbed her *raki* glass and shrugged. "Lucky guess."

She knocked back the rest of the strong, anise-flavored drink and gently placed the glass down. Her cousin stared at her the whole time. Except now, Brigham's vibes felt more like confusion and surprise than any of his usual silent warnings not to take things too far.

After noticing that both his guests had empty glasses, Burakgazi finished what was left in his, grabbed the bottle, and dutifully refilled all three drinks. "It's an interesting phrase to pull out of nowhere. It was equally as interesting when *I* heard it for the first time. I suppose, in a way, 'living records' would apply to the documentation of certain phenomena as well as the preservation of them. To my knowledge, it is merely another branch of the Order of Skrár as a whole."

"Hold on." Brigham sighed, reached for his refilled glass, and paused. "Based on what you said, that would also mean this Order of Skrár group has records on us, too. In theory. Right? Family trees. Origins." He turned to look at his cousin. "Information on the Ambrosius Clan that might not be available anywhere else."

At this point, Halsey could no longer ignore him. She knew where he was going with this. She met his gaze and clarified, "Detailed information on each member of the family, too, I bet. Dead *or* alive."

Brigham closed his eyes and drew a deep breath. Then he opened them with renewed energy and sipped his second round of *raki*.

Yep. It's already been a pain in the ass trying to prove the Blood Matriarch's back. Preparing for the bloody chaos of a war no one else is willing to accept while monsters stop doing what they're supposed to do. What the hell, though? Why not add a secret society of "living records" holding sensitive and potentially life-threatening details about our entire family and everyone in it? Sounds fun.

"I can't speak to any of *that*," Burakgazi added casually. Evidently, the cousin's silent exchange had gone over his head. He'd been too focused on refilling his drink to look at either of them. "However, I wouldn't consider anything beyond the realm of possibility for this organization. If it has even the slightest involvement with the supernatural, you can assume the Order of Skrár has a record of it somewhere."

"Wonderful." Brigham failed to keep the sarcasm from his voice, but their host seemed not to notice. Again.

"So your…sources told you about the Order of Skrár and had you contact Aydem," Halsey summarized to make sure she was lining up all the dominoes. "And Aydem's the one who recommended contracting *us*."

"*Very highly* recommended, yes. The way he spoke of your organization and your particular area of expertise left the distinct impression that the Ambrosius Clan militia is *the* expert to consult in these situations. Perhaps even the only."

Brigham clicked his tongue behind a crooked smile. "Flattering, though technically, I—"

Halsey jammed a heel into his thigh beneath the table and spoke over him. "Sounds like this Aydem really knows his stuff."

"Yes, I thought so, too."

Her cousin did fairly well at hiding whatever pain she'd caused his leg, and she only felt a little guilty about using physical force to stop him. If she'd let him keep going, he would have inadvertently hinted about other elemental families out there. The last thing any of the Clans needed was a non-magical organization of "living records" to get free information on elementals they didn't know existed.

Sucks that they know about us already, yeah. At least we can take one for the elemental team and leave it at that.

"I'd like to have a chat with this Aydem." Brigham shrugged. "Any chance you'd be willing to share his number?"

Burakgazi widened his eyes again.

Shit. Okay, I stand corrected. The last thing we need is to be indebted to a guy like this. I don't think he does favors for fun.

Halsey glanced at her cousin and shook her head. "I don't think that's necessary."

"I don't know, Hal." His tone toed the line between subtlety and making it abundantly obvious he did not agree with his partner and wouldn't back down. "There can be a lot of value in historical records. Of supernatural phenomena in all its forms. You never know when you might need a good contact who's already been vetted."

"Absolutely," Burakgazi interjected. The cousins stopped glaring at each other to look at him. "I always love to pass along a good reference. With my recommendation, of course."

"Thank you, Yusuf." Halsey nodded, but her tight, bitter smile probably didn't look all that grateful. "That's really not necessary—"

"Of course it's not. Call it...an extra token of gratitude for a job well done. I'll be more than happy to connect you with Aydem once you've successfully helped me with my little monster problem. Sound good?"

"Deal," Brigham stated before Halsey had another chance to intervene. He was clearly confident in the decision, which meant he had no idea what his partner had been up to behind his back.

Specifically that she'd already gotten the contact information for Halil Aydem from their grandmother, who had also failed to tell him about it. On purpose.

Well, this got way more convoluted than I thought possible. Definitely not looking forward to having this conversation with him one-on-one. Brigham's gonna be pissed.

"You have a monster problem," her cousin expounded as he picked up his *raki* glass again. "We have a monster solution. Let's talk about *that*."

CHAPTER ELEVEN

"As you're both clearly aware, this particular problem involves one..." Burakgazi grimaced and swirled his *raki* glass as he searched for the word he wanted. "*Uncompromising* chimera."

Brigham sniggered. "Aren't they all?"

The other man froze. "Admittedly, I don't know a thing when it comes to the characteristics of *all* chimeras. I've been told multiple times that *this* one is unique in various facets, not the least of which is its sheer hostility."

"We understand the nature of a chimera, Yusuf." Halsey nodded. "That sounds about right."

"Hmm." The man's lips twitched in an attempted smile, but now that they were getting down to business, he seemed to struggle to act like he was enjoying himself. "I suppose there's only so much I can tell you about the creature beforehand. I'm sorry to say the sum total will most likely be useless to you.

"If I had any video footage or photographic evidence, I would have brought that along. Unfortunately, none of my equipment managed to catch so much as the beast's shadow. More often than not, any attempt to record the chimera's…unusual state with visual evidence ended in equipment malfunction. If it wasn't downright destroyed, of course."

"Of course." Brigham frowned and tapped his thigh. "Hal, what do we know about chimeras and modern tech?"

"Not much." She rubbed a finger across her lips, trying to pinpoint anything she'd studied or speed-read about the creatures. "To be honest, I'm not sure there *is* anything to know about chimeras and tech."

"That's what I've been told." Burakgazi finished his *raki* and didn't wait for his guests before pouring himself a third. "I imagine you'll have the opportunity to glean quite a bit of new information from *this* one. Hopefully, it's an outlier and not some harbinger of evolutionary reactivity."

"Is that what you think this is?" Halsey asked. "A chimera that evolved the ability to break cameras from a distance?"

"I know it sounds absurd, Miss Ambrosius. At this point, I don't know *what* to think. The only thing I know is that I've run out of options for dealing with this beast on my own, and the two of you are more likely to resolve this quickly, efficiently, and completely."

"Okay, so it's insanely aggressive." Halsey spread her arms and waited for more information. When none was forthcoming, she added, "Anything else we should know before we go after it?"

Burakgazi licked his lips as he stared at his freshly poured *raki* but didn't move to drink it. "Only that the thing seems impervious to every method of disposal I've attempted so far."

"Yeah, *that* counts as important information."

"What have you tried?" Brigham prompted.

"Fire. Asphyxiation. Military-grade explosives. Steel. Ice. Skewering, stabbing, drowning. As well as burying the thing at least a mile underground with several tons of rock." When the man lifted his gaze to them again, he almost looked embarrassed to continue. "I had even planned to drop the creature from several thousand feet in the air. Incapacitated, of course. Yet the aircraft I contracted for the attempt lost all function at only a thousand feet."

Brigham stared at the man, blinked a few times, then rubbed his hands together. "I see."

"Sounds like the only thing you haven't tried is electrocution," Halsey pointed out.

"Oh no, that's also on the list."

The cousins shared a knowing look, emptier than their usual silent communication.

Well, shit. No wonder he didn't wanna give out any details until we got here in person. No one in their right mind would fly halfway across the world to take this on after hearing a list like that. If he mentions anything about already trying magic, too, we're fucked.

After a silent moment that seemed to stretch into eternity, Brigham cleared his throat. "I'm assuming this thing doesn't have flight capacity on top of everything else."

"The aircraft?"

"The chimera."

Burakgazi sighed and looked everywhere but at his

guests. "Of course. The chimera is earthbound. My apologies."

"You're doing fine."

Halsey shot him a frown. Her cousin widened his eyes and shrugged.

Yeah, the guy's obviously distressed, but it's not our job to make him feel good. He's the one who waited 'til the last second to tell us this thing's practically impossible to kill.

The fact that she'd jumped into thinking about how to kill their newest target instead of "dealing with it" formed a cold, hard lump in her throat that she swallowed with considerable effort. Killing the monsters she hunted had never been her first resort, and Halsey had spent her entire career assuming it never would be.

Yet the last monster she'd come face to face with had breathed his last with the blade of her throwing axe embedded in his chest. Right after he'd shifted into his human form from the alpha werewolf who'd not only spoken but had begged her for death.

This chimera, though… It was different.

This was a monster that didn't die.

At least, it couldn't be killed through humanity's regular means when it found something it lacked both the ability and the desire to fully understand. That was where the Ambrosius Clan came into play. Assuming Halsey and Brigham were the first elementals Burakgazi had contacted, of course.

Judging by what he'd told them so far, that was a safe assumption. Elementals were the only people on Earth who still had magic.

Or we used to be. Except ogres don't brand blood runes on

themselves, do they? I have a feeling this chimera's extra-thick skin doesn't have anything to do with evolution, either.

While another tense silence fell across the tent, Halsey focused on the cold, tight feeling that slid down her throat and into the pit of her stomach. Not to dwell on the odds stacked against them but to center her mind on something she could feel without anyone else picking up on it.

Brigham folded his arms and tapped a knuckle against his lips. He ran a hand through his messy auburn hair. "Artillery?"

Burakgazi shook his head. "No effect."

"*Airborne* artillery?"

"Munitions are no different when they're fired from the sky," Halsey muttered.

"Hey, I'm only running through a list."

"I'm not sure that's the best use of our time right now." When she looked at him again, her cousin's cheeks puffed out with a long exhale. "I think we can assume, short of dropping a nuclear weapon on this thing, Yusuf has already tried every available method."

Brigham nodded. "Available to *him*."

"Correct."

Burakgazi snorted, then tried to cover up his bitter amusement in the face of a hopeless endeavor. It didn't work too well. "I'm sorry, but I can't imagine there's much I don't have access to on my own. Yes, that does include nuclear weapons. I'm sure you understand why that's off the table."

Halsey stared at him. "No, actually. Care to explain?"

"Hal." Brigham shook his head, and she sighed.

"Sorry."

"It's quite all right." Burakgazi waved off the apology. The deep frown of concern creasing his youthful features made him look twenty years older, which felt better than listening to a thirty-year-old Turkish billionaire speaking like he was old enough to be their dad. "I understand the process. Including the necessity of frustration and the occasional venom before a suitable solution is reached. I promise I won't take it personally."

When he dipped his head toward Halsey, his smile was tight, apprehensive, and hopeless.

That's the most genuine thing he's said since we pulled up a cushion.

"Okay, then." Brigham smacked his thighs. "Thank you for the information, Yusuf. Is there anything else before we get started?"

Their host's eyes widened, and he looked between the cousins like he didn't understand a word. "Well, that's… what I'm expecting from *you*."

"We haven't seen the thing yet," Halsey replied.

"No, of course not. Forgive me. I seem to have failed in making clear the full extent of my part in this arrangement."

Halsey folded her arms and didn't try to hide a dubious frown. "Okay…"

If he calls shotgun, I'm calling this mission right now and taking us home.

Brigham stared at the other man with open curiosity, though he'd lost even the hint of a smile. None of them were smiling.

"Assuming you still want to move forward after hearing all that…" Burakgazi tilted his head and cleared his throat.

"I would never in good conscience expect anyone, even two operatives with a specialty like yours, to head out after this thing on their own—"

"Absolutely not," Halsey interrupted, shaking her head.

The man flashed her a blank, baffled stare. "I beg your pardon?"

"I'm sorry, Yusuf, but no. I know you're probably not used to hearing that, but we do draw the line somewhere."

When that still didn't sink in, Burakgazi looked at Brigham instead. "I don't quite understand."

"Right." She didn't give her cousin time to respond because he'd only try to sugarcoat things. That wouldn't do them any favors right now. "We're willing to take on this job. Sure. While that technically makes you our client, for the time being, you're also a civilian. Half our job is to keep civilians out of the fray."

Their host's face contorted further in confusion, so she figured she'd spell it out for him as plainly as possible.

"I can tell you right now that increasing our fee won't change our minds. You can't come with us."

The tent fell silent again, then Burakgazi blinked and slowly emerged from his semi-catatonic state. "Come with you..." He grabbed his *raki* glass and raised it to his lips before murmuring, "What a terrifying thought." After a quick sip, his frown had loosened, so he didn't look so entirely lost. "I have no intention of interfering with your work, Miss Ambrosius. Merely to assist you in it."

She shrugged. "Still."

"By extending the two of you absolute, unfettered access to the full extent of my personal resources. Weapons. Munitions. Machinery. Vehicles. Aircraft. Additional funds throughout the duration of this task, should you need them. I also have a rather extensive library of wartime tactics and battle strategy, though obviously, it hasn't served me nearly as successfully as I would have liked. Plus transportation, food, and lodging. All in addition to your five-hundred-thousand-dollar fee once everything is said and done."

After he'd finished rattling off the jaw-dropping list of resources at their disposal, the man looked sheepish about the whole thing as he met Halsey's gaze.

She swallowed. "Oh."

Burakgazi shrugged and lifted his glass again as he casually murmured, "*But* if you're adamant about not involving even *this* civilian in the process…"

"Not at all," Brigham blurted. "That's a fair and… reasonable offer, Yusuf."

"In addition to our fee?" Halsey asked.

"Of course." A flickering smile reappeared on the man's lips.

"No other hidden strings attached?"

"As long as we're in agreement that this little problem of mine is your highest and *only* priority, I don't see why there would be."

"What about an expiration date?" Brigham asked.

Burakgazi chuckled as his air of confidence and lavish superiority returned. He spread his arms and dipped his head in as close as he could get to a bow while sitting on a pile of cushions. "What's mine is yours for as long as it takes to get this thing done."

"Right." Brigham swallowed, then nodded with a wide grin. "Then we accept."

Burakgazi stared at Halsey and raised an eyebrow. "Miss Ambrosius?"

Great. He really thinks I'm the one who calls the shots, and Brigham's my sidekick.

Fighting not to roll her eyes, she stared back at the man and tried a smile to see how it went. Given the circumstances, it felt okay. "Brigham's my partner. If he says we accept, we accept."

"Excellent." Burakgazi snatched the frosted blue glass bottle and emptied the rest of its contents into their cups. He raised his tiny *raki* glass toward Halsey, then Brigham. "To your success."

Brigham's lips pressed together as he picked up his glass and raised it. "At this point, I can't make a better toast than that."

CHAPTER TWELVE

Three hours later, the Ambrosius cousins occupied an extensive penthouse hotel suite in the city of Adapazari, which would be their acting base of operations over the course of however long it took to kill an unkillable chimera. They'd scoured the suite and found two bedrooms with attached bathrooms, a front sitting room by the door, a living room, an enormous full-service kitchen the size of the living room, and a massive patio with an incredible view of the city.

Brigham was in high spirits again. Like they hadn't embarked on an impossible quest with half a million dollars on the line. And probably their lives.

Halsey couldn't bring herself to match his optimism. Instead, she'd parked on the gigantic, plush, eight-piece white sectional that almost felt like fur and focused on coming up with the beginning of a Plan A. The necessity for Plans B, C, and most likely D was also real, but she could only concentrate on one thing at a time.

"Dude, this is insane!" Brigham poked his head through

the sliding glass door from the patio, though she could see him through it anyway, and grinned. "Did you see this? There's a waterfall out here, Hal. Like a real waterfall just... shooting from the top of the side wall. And a *hot tub*."

"Uh-huh." With her legs pulled beneath her, she stared at the surface of the wavy, abstractly shaped, solid white marble coffee table in front of her.

"Hey." Her cousin watched her, then sighed and stepped inside. "You know, I can't help feeling like you're not loving this as much as I am right now..."

"Yeah, it's cool." She still didn't look at him. That was more time spent *not* thinking about how the hell they'd approach a chimera that didn't seem to have any weaknesses. *The only thing Burakgazi hasn't tried is magic. Fire, ice, and water have already been ticked off the list. Half the natural world at our disposal...useless. So we have air, earth, plants, and metal. What the hell are those gonna do that military-grade explosives and electrocution* can't?

"Aw, come on, Hal," Brigham whined as he crossed the open floorplan of the penthouse living room. "You can't take the rest of the day to appreciate where we are right now?"

"I appreciate it," she murmured. "I guess I'm not as thrilled about being dropped into the lap of luxury before we get our asses handed to us by *one chimera*. Or ripped apart."

"Yeesh." He grimaced and grabbed his own backside with both hands before shaking his head. "Ease up on the happy imagery, huh?"

"Want me to go for something a little darker?"

"You're hilarious." He plopped onto a piece of beige

furniture that looked like a cross between a chaise lounge and a loveseat for giants. When he spread his legs across the cushion and flopped his arms over the foot-wide ledge curving into the armrests, he looked like a two-year-old who'd climbed into his dad's chair. He exhaled heavily and turned his head toward her. "Hal."

"Brigham."

"Seriously, what are you doing?"

"I'm thinking."

"About a hundred and one ways to *not* kill a chimera? Or a hundred and one ways for us to die?"

Halsey snorted and lifted her hands to display an invisible prize on a nonexistent gameshow. "And behind door number three is…how to complete an impossible mission without destroying the whole world or your partner!"

"Ooh! Ooh! Which door should I *choose*?"

She shot him a scathing look, then they both laughed. "We got our work cut out for us on this one, cuz."

"Yeah, no shit. At least we're going into it already knowing what *doesn't* work. Plus, we're…what, ninety-five-percent sure there's only one of the things, right?"

"What?"

He blew air through loose lips. "I mean, seriously. Can you imagine if there were *nine* of them? With blood runes slapped all over their—"

"Don't." Halsey clenched her eyes shut. "My vivid imagination can only take so much."

"Oh. Right. Is that what you were doing? *Vividly imagining?*"

"That's one way to put it." She dropped her head against

the fluffy back cushion and sighed. "Best thing I can come up with so far is a strategic trial-and-error approach."

Her cousin sniggered. "Genius."

"Right?" Now that they'd started to prod the edges of talking about their mission in private, a little weight lifted from her shoulders. She smiled as she rolled her head across the back of the couch to look at him. "Hard to beat, but I'm still open to suggestions."

"Oh, yeah. Sure. Lemme whip something up for ya real quick, here…" He closed his eyes, frowned in mock concentration, and rubbed his temples. "Mmm…I'm getting…some kind of magic. Elemental, maybe. And… teamwork. Makes sense. Oh, oh. One more thing… What is it? Yup. General badassery." His hands dropped into his lap, and his hazel eyes flew open to flash optimistic intensity. "I think we're good."

"Your enthusiasm is astounding sometimes. You know that, right?"

"You're welcome."

A moment of silence stretched between them, filling the enormous suite with the kind of tension that made Halsey want to scream. Usually, she threw axes or knives at things instead. Something told her that wasn't an option here.

"Hey." Brigham's cheery tone drew her attention to him. "Don't go dark on me now, okay? Not before we've even gotten started."

"How the hell are we gonna stop this thing? I mean…*military-grade explosives.*"

"Okay, we haven't seen it in person yet, so slow your roll." He smirked and stroked the armrest fabric, idly tracking the motion of his fingers. "What *is* this stuff? Have you felt this chair?"

"Brigham."

"What?"

Halsey raised an eyebrow.

He laughed but kept fondling the soft side of the chair. "Listen. We'll go out there tomorrow, track the thing down, and test the waters, all right? Once we figure out exactly what's going on, we'll take care of this thing like we take care of everything else. A-Team forever."

"I'm not saying that."

"Come on, cuz. It's a catchphrase. Everybody needs one."

"Not that one."

"Well, shit." Brigham rolled his eyes and slumped back against the chair. "What would *you* choose?"

Halsey mimed pulling a weapon from her belt, taking aim, and tossing an invisible blade at him.

"For the love of— That's not a catchphrase, Hal. It's gratuitous violence."

"Oh, really? So saying a catchphrase *before* cutting someone down makes it *less* violent?"

"It does when they hear the catchphrase and know what's coming if they don't get lost pretty damn quick. Then it's giving them a *choice*."

"How do they know what the catchphrase means?"

He widened his eyes and leaned over the seat cushion, which stretched farther in front of him than his fully extended legs. "Because it *catches*. Then it spreads. By word of mouth, because people remember that shit. It's right there in the word."

She glanced at the high ceiling and pretended to consider his argument. "Yeah, but we fight monsters."

"That's—" Brigham lifted a finger as his mouth popped open, then he wrinkled his nose. "Yeah. That *does* make it hard for them to understand what we're saying. Not to mention remember it so they can pass it along to their friends. Shit."

"Well, *one* of them might," Halsey muttered a split second before she realized what she'd said.

"What was that?"

"Nothing." She chuckled, shook her head, and tried to play it off like she was messing around.

Bad time to be careless and start dropping bombs like that, Halsey. He still doesn't know about the alpha werewolf named Rolfr who can talk. Or who could, *anyway...*

With everything facing them in their immediate, mission-pending future, keeping secrets from her cousin seemed pointless. Like the truth about that haunting interaction with the silverback alpha in Ireland.

Except telling him about it would make him question my sanity all over again. Then I'd have to explain I was already looking for Aydem behind his back when we got here. Who we're apparently gonna meet with after we get this freak chimera to bite the dust. How am I supposed to spill the beans all at once about that one, too?

Her cousin's stare burned into the side of her face, so she faced him with a deadpan expression. "What?"

"You, my friend, are *way* too uptight."

"You're a little too unconcerned about this."

"Correction." Brigham thrust a finger in the air. "I know when, where, and how to compartmentalize. Tomorrow, we hit the ground running after this dickhead monster that won't die. Yet. But *today*..."

"If you say anything about tours, clubbing, yucking it up with the locals without speaking a lick of Turkish, or window-shopping, I'm gonna stop you right there."

"Me?" He slapped a hand to his chest in mock insult. "Honestly, Halsey, I find that appalling." Then the full extent of her words sank in, and he dropped his hand. "Wait, there are actual clubs here? Like *club*-clubs?"

"Kill me now."

"Come on. I'm screwing with you, cuz. What I *actually* have in mind is so much better. And cooler. And less embarrassing. For you."

"Oh, gee. Was I supposed to be offended by that?"

Brigham laughed as he tried to stand from the chair. The sound cut short when he discovered he couldn't get to the floor without scooting another two feet across the cushion. "Damn it. What the hell kinda person would... This chair sucks."

The sight of her grown cousin fighting with a chair made Halsey snigger, and he shot her a scathing glare before making it to his feet.

Then he tugged down the bottom hem of his shirt, smoothed the front down, and cleared his throat. "Tonight, we feast!"

"No." She shook her head and raised both hands. "I had more than enough in Burakgazi's tent. And it's...what? Not even five o'clock."

Brigham's shoulders slumped. "Figure of speech, Hal. What, you think I'd *enjoy* ordering an entire eight-course meal from a five-star tasting menu for each of us? With wine pairings? On someone else's dime?"

Her jaw dropped until it hung completely open. "You did not."

He wiggled his eyebrows, then laughed. "Hell, no. That's for *after* we bag the immortal chimera. I did get us a little something, and I think you're really gonna—"

A sharp, brisk knock came at the penthouse's front door, and his wide-eyed excitement made him look like a five-year-old who'd caught an up-close glimpse of his hero at Disneyland.

"Here we go." With a giddy grin, Brigham rubbed his hands together and headed for the door.

"What, Brigham?" she called after him, turning on the couch to watch him scamper off. "I'm gonna *what*?"

"Well, now you gotta wait for it." He laughed maniacally and skipped the rest of the way toward the door before collecting himself.

Halsey gave up trying to peek and faced forward on the couch to sink back into the luxuriously soft cushions. *If I were here with anyone else, I'd probably be excited about a surprise. But it's Brigham. And a surprise.*

Another man's low voice traveled across the penthouse, interspersed with Brigham's enthusiastic, "Oh, *man*. This is perfect. Yeah, yeah, for sure. You know what? Here. Totally. You bet, man. Have a good night."

She winced as she tried to imagine what he could have possibly ordered, paid for, and had brought up to the penthouse *for* them. That alone was something her cousin would definitely get excited about, and it didn't help her imagination settle on anything he was likely to show her in the next few seconds.

The front door shut with an echoing click, followed by rustling paper that sounded way too thick to be a paper bag.

Is that a gift bag? And...tissue paper?

"Yes!" Brigham's giddy squeak, followed by a high-pitched cackle, made her more concerned about what she'd find if she looked over the back of the couch.

Instead, she slid down and slouched as far as she could go until her heels skimmed the polished wooden floor beneath her.

If there was ever a time for him to play his worst joke ever, now would be it.

"Hal! Get ready, cuz. This shit is off the chain!"

Her eyes flew open. "Don't say that."

"What?"

"Seriously, do you know *anyone* who says that?"

His sharp laugh echoed across the entire penthouse. "Yeah. Me."

After that came the urgent banging of Brigham opening and closing the kitchen cabinets and drawers. Silverware rattled around. The same sound of tissue paper in a gift bag followed, then one loud *pop* and a muffled curse.

"You okay in there?"

"Yeah...gimme one sec." Something else sounded like cardboard ripping, then thin plastic crinkling, then sharp plastic snaps, followed by more rummaging around in the kitchen. "Oh, yeah..."

Oh, no.

CHAPTER THIRTEEN

Halsey grimaced and stayed slumped against the couch, as if slinking below the furniture line would make her cousin forget she was there. It took her a few seconds to notice the sudden, absolute silence filling the penthouse.

Parents talk about the dreaded silence with little kids, but I have him...

Halsey waited a little longer, then tentatively called out. "Brigham?"

Nothing.

Either he's dead, or he's playing one hell of a practical joke. Which means I'll hate it, and I might kill him.

Moving like she was trying not to scare off a scurrying little critter, she turned and crawled across the couch, then pulled herself up until she knelt against the back cushions. Only half the kitchen was visible from this part of the living room, but she tried to peer around the corner anyway. "You, uh... You coming back in here, or—"

"Ta-da!"

"Fuck!" She lurched off the couch with a wild swing,

and her magic inadvertently snagged the keys to their rental car lying on the marble coffee table. They flew off the table with a violent jingle and headed directly for her cousin's cheesy grin.

Brigham's only reaction was to jerk his head aside and take half a step in the same direction. The keys whizzed by his head before striking the living room wall behind him.

Two of them went through the plaster, and the rest of the keys attached to the ring jingled and clacked against the wall.

"Shit on a pickle, Hal!" Brigham spun halfway around to stare at the keys in the wall, then turned toward her and burst out laughing.

Halsey sat back on her heels and glared at him. "Really?"

"You really thought… And then you—" He cracked up again and doubled over as he staggered toward the coffee table, trying not to drop the armload of whatever he was carrying. Which she still couldn't see. "What the… Ha!" Several glass-sounding somethings clinked onto the table, followed by a mass of black plastic lumps.

She was only vaguely aware of what he was laying out because she couldn't tear her gaze from the wall-keys.

"Go*damn*! I'd ask what's making you so uptight, but that seems like a never-ending list."

"I'm fine."

"Dude…" Brigham gasped a breath and shifted his laughter into chuckling as he stood upright, his arms empty once more. "You tried to start my face with the car keys."

"You—" Halsey pressed her lips together and fought a

laugh, but she couldn't keep it from her voice. "You know I don't like surprises."

"I've heard about chicks using car keys between their knuckles, like, for self-defense and shit, but that was...*aggressive*."

"Yeah, well, the last time you snuck up on me, I was pulling glitter from every crevice in my body for a month."

Her cousin howled laughter. "That was like *ten years* ago!"

"And it scarred me forever. Maybe literally." Still choking back her own laughter and not knowing why she felt it necessary, Halsey focused her magic on the car keys and flicked her fingers. The metal ripped from the wall, widening the holes they'd already made. Chunks of plaster and drywall toppled to the floor as the keys flew into her open hand. When she closed her fist around the key ring, the sharp ends of the keys poked out from between her knuckles.

She smirked and turned toward her cousin with a joke about brass knuckles on her lips. That was when she realized the burbling trickle of pouring liquid filed the room. She saw what Brigham was actually doing.

"Champagne." She lowered her key-knuckled hand, then tossed the ring onto the coffee table. "That's what this whole thing was building up to?"

"That's only the start." He finished filling a ridiculously fragile champagne flute with bubbly golden liquid and handed it over. Then he picked up the second one, stepped between the coffee table and Halsey kneeling on the couch, and poured his own drink. "Man, look at the head on *this...*"

"I don't think that's how you judge the quality of champagne, dude."

"It's not?"

Halsey guffawed. "It's not *beer*."

"I know that." He stared at the bubbling surface of his drink and shrugged. "So, how do you tell?"

"I don't know. I mean, with wine, it's like…watching the legs."

Brigham sniggered. "You're tellin' *me*."

"No, the *legs*. Like how it runs back down the side of the—forget it. I don't think that applies here. Generally, with champagne, you can tell by the price."

He lifted his head from sniffing his drink and grinned. "Well, then, lemme tell ya. This stuff is *real* good."

"Brigham." She stared at him, and he ignored her chastising look as he tipped his head back and made a big show of trying the first sip.

"Ah…" He smacked his lips a few times, then turned the corners of his mouth down and held the glass aloft in an impression of a snob. "*Crisp*."

"Uh-huh. Does it taste expensive?"

"Quite."

"How expensive?" She was hesitant to ask, and the look in his eye made her wish she hadn't.

Brigham lifted a shoulder and turned away from her in a playful snub. "An even two."

"*Hundred?*"

"Thousand." He wiggled his eyebrows, raised the champagne flute to his lips, and murmured, "Per bottle."

Halsey almost dropped her glass. "Are you shitting me?"

"Nope."

"How many bottles did you—"

"As many as we can drink. Tonight."

"Brigham!"

He laughed and walked across the living room before spinning back around, careful not to slosh his expensive champagne all over as he spread his arms. "Come on, Hal. We're on vacation. All expenses paid!"

"The hell we are…"

"We are *tonight*. Did I mention the all-expenses-paid part?" He sipped again, then closed his eyes in bliss. "You need to relax and enjoy it."

"By charging thousands of dollars in champagne to Burakgazi's credit card the first night we're here? What is *wrong* with you?"

"Right now? Absolutely nothing. Drink it."

"Dude."

"He gave us a *limitless credit card* and said to 'use it at will.' Like, those exact words."

Halsey hardly felt the glass in her hand anymore as she shook her head in disbelief. "It's a broad generalization, man. Meaning whatever we need *for the job*."

"Huh. Seemed pretty specific to me."

"And how the hell are we supposed to explain champagne as a business expense?"

"Hey, you saw his face when we started talking about the chimera, right?" He grabbed her empty hand and hauled her off the couch as delicately as possible without making her spill the bubbly. "If he couldn't even *talk* about it sober, you think he expects us to go through this whole mission without a drink? At all?"

"Spending more money on booze doesn't get you

drunker."

"Ha! Says who?" Brigham slung an arm around her shoulders and guided her toward the massive penthouse kitchen.

"I'm talking about comparable volume here, and you know it."

"Aw. It's so cute when you say nerdy stuff."

Halsey jagged her free hand into his ribs under his armpit, and her cousin squealed before jerking his arm off her shoulders and jumping away. *"That* was cute."

"Fine. Agree to disagree, okay?"

"No. Not agree. Not okay." When her cousin sniggered at her passionately incorrect grammar, she scrunched her nose and tried to shake off how weird it was to hear *herself* say that. "Seriously, Brigham, if we can't—"

"Stop. Lemme stop you right there, Hal." For added emphasis, Brigham jumped in front of his cousin and blocked her path to the kitchen. "'Cause you're right about a few things but missed the mark with the *how.*"

"Huh?"

"I know, right?" He wiggled his eyebrows again, then eyed her champagne flute, which she continued to refuse to drink. Brigham rolled his eyes and sipped from his glass. "Okay. You're right. We can't write any of this shit off as a business expense."

"Right."

"Not that our *generous benefactor* is gonna ask us for an itemized receipt when he's got a dead chimera in his yard. But still."

"But still." Halsey nodded. "So you're gonna return all this stuff and get the charges reversed."

"Uh...no." He spun again and headed toward the granite kitchen island that was as big as any dining room table. "They're business expenses."

"Okay. I love you. But in about three seconds, I'm gonna take you down, take the credit card, and tell Burakgazi thanks but no thanks—"

"They're *his*." Brigham grinned and spread his arms again. "Eh? Right?"

Halsey blinked. "His what?"

"Business expenses, Hal. That's how taxes work. Don't tell me you've been letting me do your taxes for the last five years because you thought I'd screw 'em up."

"I... No. You're good at those."

"Aw, thanks." He chuckled at her exasperated glower and drank more champagne. "Listen, Burakgazi wants us to spend his money for two reasons. That I know of. First, he's gotta keep us *happy*, right? We could go out and buy a bunch of machine guns and RPGs and...I don't know. A hundred fucking axes if you wanted, but we already know that's a massive waste. And *he* knows the two best monster hunters in the world—"

"That the Ambrosius Clan has to offer..."

"*In the world* are gonna be operating at peak performance when they feel like they have everything they need. Plus a lot of what they want. In case you didn't notice, cuz, we're doing the guy a hell of a favor."

"Worth half a million."

"Meh. Tit for tat." Brigham pretended not to notice when she cracked up laughing and kept talking over her instead. "Either way, we're literally his last resort. He can't afford to lose our interest. He *can* afford to buy our happiness and continued comfort until this whole thing is over. Yeah, I know people say money can't *buy* you happiness, but I'm a firm believer in exceptions to every rule—"

"Hey." Halsey snapped her fingers in his face, then pointed at her own eyes. "Focus."

"Yep. Thanks. *Second* reason." He held up two fingers and grinned like a man who'd discovered the secrets to the universe and everything else.

Yikes. He looks as nuts as everyone else thinks Meemaw and I are.

Brigham continued. "The more we spend, the bigger our new friend's tax write-off. He's entertaining potential business partners."

Halsey wrinkled her nose yet stared at the champagne in her hand, wondering how it tasted. "Okay, if we *didn't* have mission orders from the Council and had to be here anyway, we've already sat down with him and said we'll take the job. The 'potential' part's over."

"Is it? There's no contract, and we haven't actually received a cent of payment. Only a promise of what we'll get in exchange for *our* promise of doing what we gotta do to get paid. Technically, we're not his business partners until that freaky-ass chimera eats shit and Burakgazi hands us a check. Tax. Write-off." He mimed scribbling midair, then pulled away the invisible pen and blew on it like it was a gun barrel instead.

Halsey could only stare at her cousin in blank disbelief. Then she giggled, widened her eyes, and gazed around the kitchen. "Holy shit."

"Bet that champagne tastes pretty fucking good *now*, huh?"

Halsey didn't waste a second more before taking a long, slow sip from her first-ever glass of two-thousand-dollar champagne. She closed her eyes, inhaled through her nose, and waited for the bubbly tingle on the roof of her mouth to subside.

"And the winner is..." Still grinning, Brigham spread his arms and walked backward toward the kitchen island.

"Yep." She held out her glass to study the drink under the kitchen light and snorted. "Okay. I totally get it now."

"Damn right you do." Her cousin smacked the countertop, then gazed pointedly at the center of the island. "Now feast your eyes..."

It took her a moment to figure out what she was looking at, mostly because it was still partially packaged. "What's this? Charcuterie board. Nice."

"Thank you."

"Ooh. Fresh olive oil and balsamic from—*hey*. Just a hop, skip, and a jump away, right?"

"Last I checked, Italy hasn't moved, no." Brigham drank more champagne, looking incredibly pleased with himself.

"That bread smells freaking amazing."

"From right down the street, apparently. Best in town."

"A whole tray of chocolate truffles. Wow. Plus this little weird-looking can of..." Halsey snatched the container, which at first she'd thought contained chewing tobacco. That would have been out of character for either of them. Then she took a closer look at the label. "Caviar."

Her cousin repeatedly sniggered in a way that reminded her of a bully character in a kids' cartoon.

"You actually ordered caviar and had it brought to the *penthouse...*" She didn't mean for it to sound like a groaning complaint, but it did. She wasn't sure what she'd meant it to sound like, anyway.

"Bet you never thought you'd say *that* and actually mean it, huh?"

"Dude, this whole situation is one first after another." After dropping the caviar can onto the kitchen island, she studied the ridiculously expensive spread, then frowned. "Everyone involved in the process of getting this up here is gonna think we're a couple after this. You know that, right?"

Brigham scoffed, downed the rest of his champagne, and tore open the delicate cellophane gift-wrapping around the charcuterie plate. "That's ridiculous."

"Do you *see* what you bought us? For dinner?"

"Do *you* see any roses anywhere? No. Trust me, I skipped the chocolate-covered strawberries. Don't make it weird, cuz." He snatched a wad of thinly sliced prosciutto, threw his head back, and dropped the whole thing in his mouth. "Whoa. This is…holy shit. You need that."

Halsey laughed as she watched him digging into the meat-and-cheese board that was supposed to be for two people, then rolled her eyes. "Aw, what the hell?"

"That's what I'm talkin' about! Okay, grab stuff and take it into the living room."

"Like what?"

"Pick a thing, Hal. Anything. Living room. Go."

"Okay…" She shot him a confused look as they piled their dinner of hors d'oeuvres into their arms. Then she paused when she noticed the black cardboard box at the far end of the kitchen island. "What's that?"

"That's why we're going to the living room. Well, that

and the champagne I left in there. Whoops. Come on."

"You know the box is empty, right?"

"It wasn't when it got here. Less talking, more doing." He shooed her out of the kitchen and grabbed another bottle of champagne from the fridge.

Halsey moved as quickly as she could back to the living room and laughed when she saw the proof. "No way."

"Oh, come on. You didn't think I paid for an empty box, did you? Or a mislabeled surprise?"

She carefully set down a tray of chocolate and a still-warm, bagged loaf of fresh bread, then downed the rest of her first drink and placed the empty glass on the coffee table. After that, it seemed almost too good to be true when she reached for the rectangular piece of tech covered in hard black plastic. The logo on the side was unmistakable.

"I can't believe you did this," she stated with a laugh.

"Oh, yeah. There's this, too." Brigham whipped the final surprise from behind his back and tossed the game box onto the marble coffee table beside the console.

Halsey grinned. "You got us *Blood Lust*."

"Uh-huh."

"You're insane."

"You know what? If two-thousand-dollar bottles of champagne, a helluva spread like this, and the newest version of our favorite game console *with* the newest release of our favorite game make me insane, then yeah. Okay. I'll take it."

She suddenly felt much better about their first night in Turkey. "You and me both, cuz."

He didn't have to do anything else but pour her another glass of champagne.

CHAPTER FOURTEEN

After a literal night of champagne and caviar, more fun hanging out with her cousin than they'd had in a long time thanks to videogames, and eating every speck of food, Halsey was surprised at how good she felt when she crawled into the king-sized bed in her own private bedroom of the penthouse suite. She'd managed to table her concerns and frustrations about the unkillable chimera for the night, so she didn't have any trouble slipping off to sleep minutes after she'd pulled the comforter up over her head.

Staying asleep was a different story.

She had no idea what time it was when a low, humming buzz and intermittent flashes of strobing light roused her from a deep sleep. The silence and almost complete darkness of the penthouse had made it easy to get comfy and sleepy, but the sound and the light were impossible to ignore.

The buzzing only seemed to grow louder as the flashes of light moved back and forth across her closed eyelids.

Halsey growled and tossed the comforter off before slapping a hand onto the nightstand. There was her phone, cold and solid against her palm, and she stabbed it to get rid of whatever ludicrous alarm she'd apparently set during her fun night with Brigham.

But it wasn't her alarm because the buzzing wouldn't shut up, and the lights kept blinding her from a direction that wasn't her phone.

"Seriously?"

She slapped her phone down, then pushed herself up so she could get to that damn noise.

Another brilliant flash of light crossed her eyes. She clenched them shut and flinched away as she raised an arm to shield herself. The buzzing continued, and the next time the flashing light passed over her, she blocked it enough with her open hand to see what it was.

The light was a deep crimson, dark enough to make her think of blood yet bright enough to rouse her from one of the best nights of sleep she'd had in a while.

The disturbance seemed to be coming from the middle of the bedroom. She only figured out that much because after the last pass of the light failed to blind her, she watched the beam of crimson circle the perimeter of her room like a laser scanner.

I swear, if Brigham added some useless, stupidly expensive security system that's gonna wake me up like this every night...

Once she shook herself awake enough to stand without falling, Halsey shuffled across the enormous bedroom toward the door. She felt the wall for the light switch and angrily clicked it on.

The brightness that flooded her room from the overhead lights wasn't nearly as bright as the mystery laser beam, but it was constant and glaring. The back of her eyes hurt before they adjusted to the new glare. As her vision focused and she made out the source of the crimson light and the buzzing, she almost wished she'd kept the light off.

The copper orb hovered in the air like it had a month ago in her grandmother's living room. Though this time, there were more than a few differences.

For one, Halsey had no idea the thing could make any noise at all. The blinding sliver of crimson light coming from *inside* the small sphere made it even worse.

Blood-red for blood magic, right? Screw this.

Disturbed at the thought, knowing the Blood Matriarch's coffin had disappeared from the storage unit where she'd found the sand, she growled and stomped toward the floating orb.

"Nope. Nuh-uh. We're not doing this right now. We're not doing this *ever*. You're done."

The last thing she'd expected was an actual response from the object.

After her final, facetious command left her mouth, the orb stopped whatever it was doing. The buzzing hum cut off abruptly. The crimson light continued circling the room for another half-rotation, flickered, then blinked.

The orb itself remained in the literal middle of the room.

Okay, now *it looks like it did at Meemaw's.*

Halsey sighed, snatched the sphere from the air, and paused. The thing didn't offer any resistance. It felt as cold, smooth, and *almost* natural as it had when resting in her jacket pocket. It didn't glow, hum, or warm at her touch like she would've anticipated if she hadn't been half-asleep and a hundred percent pissed.

"I don't know *what* I thought I'd get out of you," she hissed as she spun and headed for the walk-in closet. "I'm drawing the line at…whatever the hell that was, though."

The closet door swung open to thump against the bedroom wall. Halsey stalked inside, stooped, and grabbed the plain black duffel bag she'd slid beneath the lowest shelf.

"I know I should've taken you out of my jacket the second Brigham called dibs on the other bedroom." The air rippled with the sharp, violent sound of the bag's zipper when she tugged it open. "But *no*. It's only a ball of copper, Hal. Don't worry about it, Hal. Something you made could never be such a *pain in the ass* when you're trying to sleep, think, or plan potentially deadly engagement tactics for an impossible mission."

She paused, glaring down at the orb. To her utter dismay, she realized she'd stopped ranting only because this was the part where the other party usually said something in reply.

In this case, the other party was an inanimate copper ball.

"Great. See? Now I'm talking to a hunk of metal and getting disappointed when it doesn't talk back." She shoved the orb among the other contents of the duffel bag, which happened to be her throwing axes, two extra utility knives, and a cache of personal firearms and supernatural munitions. She didn't necessarily intend to use them all but had brought them along for the ride anyway.

The orb clinked and clanked against barrels, stocks, and

spare magazines. She fumbled around in the suitcase she hadn't bothered to unpack for a pair of socks and used those to stuff the copper ball deep into the corner of the duffel bag.

"That's where you're staying until you—until *I* can figure out what the hell to do with you." She'd almost said, "until you learn to behave," but that was insane.

Halsey noted the icky feeling of having snapped in anger the way *she'd* been snapped at for so long, years before she'd learned how to snap back. She shook it off before forcefully zipping the duffel bag up again. Then she stood and slid the whole thing under the bottom shelf with the ball of her foot.

The only logical thing to do after that was step back, dust off her hands, and stare at her weapons bag for what felt like an eternity.

"I'm not crazy," she murmured. "If I'd heard the thing *talking back* to me, *that* would make me crazy."

After backing out of the walk-in closet, Halsey massaged her hands. She couldn't take her eyes off the bag.

"Hiding from a copper ball would make me crazy, too. So I'm definitely not doing *that*."

She paused again, then peeled her gaze from the bag for a split second so she could see the closet door before she grabbed it and swung it shut. It whispered across the wooden floors on its well-oiled hinges and closed with a soft little *click*.

She released a heavy breath and nodded. "That's right. You heard me. Don't even think about—"

A loud, abrupt knock on her bedroom door made her jump and suck in a hissing breath.

"Hal?" Brigham called from the other side.

She stood still, clenching her eyes shut and trying not to breathe too loudly in the hopes that he might walk away.

"Hal, I know you're in there, and I know you're up. Your light's on."

"Just a sec," she called back, then grimaced because what could she possibly have needed another second *for*?

Can't sweep this one under the rug, can you? If you don't open the door to meet him head-on, he's definitely gonna think something's up. Because it is. I think.

To make it more believable, she waited a few more seconds in silence before casually striding across the room to open the bedroom door. When she propped herself up with one hand against the doorframe, she didn't have to pretend to be tired enough to rub her eyes. "What's up?"

His usually messy auburn hair stuck up in all directions, helped into the style by a significant amount of static. He wore his flannel pajama pants and nothing else. He searched his cousin's face with bleary eyes, then tried to peer past her into the bedroom. "You good in there?"

"Yep. I had to pee." The second she said it, she kicked herself for not thinking that through first. The ensuite bathroom was on the opposite side of the room from the walk-in closet.

Let's hope he doesn't start thinking too hard about what side of the room he heard my voice coming from. If I get busted for one lie, I might as well get busted for all of them, right?

Brigham didn't look convinced enough to leave it alone, and his groggy frown deepened. "You sure?"

"Uh-huh."

"'Cause you sounded really pissed off a few seconds ago."

Halsey rolled her eyes. "Yeah, well, you'd be pissed off if your first night of good sleep in *months* got interrupted by something as stupid as a...full bladder." The words hardly made any sense, but she pursed her lips and shook her head, attempting to be more compelling. To both of them.

"Huh." Her cousin scrutinized her, then shrugged and scratched the back of his head. "Yeah. I mean, you *did* wet the bed 'til you were ten."

"No, dude." She glared at him. "That was you."

"Wait..." His confusion morphed into a crooked smile, and he chuckled. "Oh, yeah. That *was* me."

"Okay. As fun as this is right now, I *really* wanna get back to sleep. So..."

"Right. Yeah. Okay—" Brigham sucked in a sharp breath and opened his mouth in an enormous yawn, then stretched his arms above his head. Halsey found herself yawning in response as he scratched his bare belly and smacked his lips. "Well, next time you gotta do the deed, man, keep it down, all right? You'd think it'd be quiet all the way across the entire penthouse, but there's some kinda crazy echo in here or something. I can hear *everything.*"

If he'd still been looking at her, he would have seen the color disappear from her face before flooding back in with a darker flush. Yet Brigham had already turned and shuffled halfway back to the other bedroom by the time he'd finished talking.

He's talking about all the "noises." He heard your voice, not the actual words. There's no way he heard you talking to a hunk of magical metal and hid it that believably. Brigham's not that good at lying.

She heard his bedroom door whisper closed at the other end of the suite before the ensuing click.

But I am.

She grimaced, closed her bedroom door, and scanned her silent, empty bedroom for any other signs of something gone magically haywire.

There were none.

Okay, once we figure out how to take care of Burakgazi's psycho chimera, I'm coming clean. About everything. He already thinks I'm nuts, but he's still here.

Making a plan for when she would reveal all the little truths to her cousin soothed at least some of her guilt over lying to him for the last month. That made it easy for Halsey to slap off the overhead light, stumble across the bedroom one more time, and flop into the dreamlike king-sized bed for another few hours of incredible sleep.

CHAPTER FIFTEEN

After taking a night to settle into their Adapazari penthouse, Halsey and Brigham were ready to get down to business the next morning. They ordered an enormous breakfast delivered to their suite, and the personal buffet served as the fuel for their morning brainstorming.

The massive carafe of amazing coffee didn't hurt, either.

"Okay, here's how I think we should approach this." Halsey took a massive, crunching bite of her second perfectly crisped slice of toast slathered with melted butter and jam.

"I'm all ears, cuz." Brigham held the coffee toward her and filled her giant mug again when she nodded. "Pass the smoked salmon."

She slid the tray across the table, then fixed her coffee the way she liked it. "We can already cross everything we know the chimera *doesn't* do off the list."

"Yeah, like *die*. So far, that's a pretty short list."

"Not when we include all the things it doesn't respond to."

"Oh, okay. Yeah." He shrugged as he loaded a bit of everything onto a massive round of Turkish *pide* bread, then lifted it toward his face with both hands. "That's a longer list, then."

"Uh-huh." Halsey chewed slowly and watched her cousin eat his breakfast like a man half-starved and completely lacking taste buds. "Burakgazi seems to think this thing is way more aggressive than any other chimera, based on his 'sources.'"

"Yeah, not being killed by all the shit he threw at it? That'd make anyone aggressive." When Brigham swallowed his overflowing mouthful of food, the sound was loud enough to make Halsey pause in the middle of dishing cherries, strawberries, and sweet melon onto her plate. He smacked his lips, spilling crumbs all over his side of the table, then reached for the orange juice. "Can't even shoot it down *from* the sky. Bullets don't change 'cause they're fired from the air, right?"

"Yeah, we established that." She stabbed a piece of melon with her fork, popped it into her mouth, and chewed thoughtfully. "Now we need a list of what we can safely assume about chimeras in general."

"Why? This isn't a normal chimera."

"I'm working through a process, Brigham. Go with it."

He pulled a platter of various types of meat toward him and shrugged. "Fair enough. You want legends or facts?"

"All of it."

"Well, if we didn't have a good word like *chimera* for it, it'd be a lion-goat-snake…thing."

"How clever."

"Thanks." Brigham smirked before downing an entire glass of orange juice and digging back into his food. "Plus, they've got three heads. Business-lion in the front, party-snake in the back."

Halsey snorted. "That's two heads. Are you describing a monster or a haircut?"

"Maybe both. Made all the more badass and weird as hell by the fire-breathing goat-head parasite *on* its back. Head number three."

"You know, part of me thinks Burakgazi didn't put much time and effort into his research, if fire was one of his attempted methods of disposal."

"Hey, the guy got desperate. It happens."

After slowly sipping more coffee, Halsey frowned at the bits of breakfast food she'd already tried littering her plate. "We did ask him about airstrikes, though."

"Yeah. *You* said bullets don't—"

"I know what I said about bullets. Now I'm thinking about the legends, right? Greek mythology."

"Right. Dude got sent out by Poseidon to kill the thing, but it was a setup. Or at least it was supposed to be." Brigham raised a clawed hand toward the ceiling and bellowed, "Enter the mighty Pegasus!"

"I haven't had nearly enough coffee yet for this," Halsey muttered through a smirk.

"Well, get with the program, cuz. Drink up." Brigham scanned the table for the next course of what was sure to be his usual three- to four-course breakfast. "Dude would've gotten his guts smeared across the land if it wasn't for the flying horse. Who apparently was friends with, like, *all* the Greek heroes. Cool, I guess, but it kinda makes you wonder where the thing's loyalties really were, you know?"

"Probably with making sure those heroes didn't get murdered by their own families." She held back a laugh watching her cousin stuff his face as she picked at her plate. "Dude's name was Bellerophon, by the way. And Poseidon was his dad."

"Damn." Brigham gulped his mouthful and stared at the table as he considered what they'd learned during militia training, which he'd obviously forgotten. He laughed wryly. "We thought *our* family was bad. Talk about secrets and betrayal, am I right?"

His off-the-cuff comment hit her like a ton of bricks, and a hot flush erupted up the sides of her neck and into her cheeks. *Pull it together. He's not talking about you, and you know it. Focus on the job and the plan.*

"Right," she muttered, staring at her plate. "Families."

He looked at her as he chewed more food, studying her face with a knowing smile for what felt like a long time. At last, he poured more juice, glugged down half the glass, and dove back into their brainstorming session. "So that bit's weird, then, right? Weirder than normal, anyway."

"What bit?"

"That our oh-so-resourceful client thought to try airstrikes, and they didn't work."

Halsey shrugged. "I'm pretty sure Bellerophon and Pegasus didn't have a whole lot of access to military aircraft and high-caliber ammunition."

"True." Brigham half-stood from his chair so he could

reach the platter of Turkish pastries, then sifted through them by hand, hunting for the one he wanted.

Halsey didn't bother reminding him their room-service breakfast was supposed to be for *both* of them. Partly because she wouldn't want any of the pastries he'd gotten his fingers all over anyway and partly because the food was distracting enough that he hadn't noticed her odd reaction to his comment about familial lies and betrayal.

"So how *did* the chimera-murdering duo manage to, you know...murder the chimera?"

She chuckled and drank more coffee. "Arrows from the sky. That only weakened the thing, of course."

"Oh, yeah. Of course."

"The mortal blow was from a lead spear."

Her cousin finally found his desired pastry. He plopped back in his chair and took a crunching, gooey-jam-filled bite. "Really? That's all it took?"

"Do you remember *any* of the six months we spent on the monsters of Greek mythology?"

"In Ambrosius militia school? Dude, that was forever ago." Brigham licked the fruit jam off his fingers and shrugged. "Hey, I remembered Pegasus, though."

"Yeah, you and every kid who's ever seen the *Hercules* movie." Halsey watched him noisily guzzle down the first pastry before he snatched up a second. "In a way, the chimera technically destroyed itself. Lead spear in the goat-head's throat. Then, because the goat-head was the one that breathed fire..."

"That's *right*." He snapped his fingers and pointed at her. "Goat-head's fire melted the spear. So the dumb thing actually swallowed molten lead and burned up all *three* heads from the inside out. And the body, obviously."

"Obviously."

"Kinda gives us the upper hand, right? With the lead spear."

She snorted. "Oh, did *you* pack one? I must've missed that in all the other giant, six-foot weapons we brought with us to Turkey."

"No…" Her cousin rolled his eyes and jammed more pastry into his mouth. "The lead part. Metal. Elemental magic. Ambrosius specialty. You feel me?"

"Under normal circumstances, I'd agree. These aren't normal circumstances, though."

"You don't say."

Halsey drummed her fingers on the table as she mentally walked through the list of things they'd marked, mentioned, and heard about chimeras in general and this one in particular. "I'm pretty sure if the molten-lead theory had any merit, an aerial strike with military-grade munitions against a beast as pissed off and violent as this one would've pumped the thing *full* of molten lead. Ten times over. That's obviously a non-starter. Plus, I don't think the solution's gonna be that simple."

"It could be." After tossing back yet another glass of orange juice, Brigham leaned back in his chair. He released a trembling belch, then grabbed his coffee mug and held it in both hands as if they were trying to get warm next to a winter fire.

When he didn't continue the thought, Halsey clicked her tongue and nodded. "Wanna elaborate on that?"

"I'm processing." He stared blankly at the edge of the

table, his eyes narrowing and widening as he went through whatever mental process required this much silence and concentration. Then he sniffed, sighed, and nodded once. "Okay, we're good."

"Great."

He continued. "We don't have a giant lead spear of mythological proportions, even Greek ones. Yet, assuming that's the way to kill the thing, maybe the problem *is* as simple as figuring out the right molten-lead theory. Not with bullets, from the ground *or* from the sky. Obviously. Bullets are too spread out. Yes, even with fully automatic weapons. They're basically pellets for this monster douche."

"Huh." Halsey frowned as she considered the implications. "So you're saying we try something halfway between bullets and an epic spear."

"Yeah. Exactly. We don't even *need* a Pegasus. Only a few extra skills my dude Bellerophon didn't have, and Burakgazi definitely doesn't."

"I'm pretty sure Burakgazi doesn't know about magic at all, honestly. Except for the monsters."

"Well, yeah. Lucky for us, the thing that kills the chimera in all the stories happens to be the Ambrosius Clan's *coup d'état.*"

Halsey pressed her lips together to hold back a laugh. "Nope."

"What? That's right."

"It's *coup de grace,* cuz. 'Blow of mercy.'"

"The death strike. Yeah." He glanced around the penthouse dining room, then flicked his gaze toward her. "What'd *I* say?"

"Violently overthrowing a government. Like a mutiny but without the ships-and-sailors part."

"Huh." Brigham scratched the back of his head. "Hell, it might be time for one of those, too. Know what I'm sayin'?"

"Let's not get too far ahead of ourselves." Halsey sipped her coffee, thinking of all the ways they could get their hands on enough solid metal to try melting it down any number of the chimera's throats. *If that doesn't work, we'll go right back to the drawing board.* "First, we take care of this chimera. Then we can think about how to change the way the Ambrosius Clan does things."

"Done. Right after I nom the rest of these pastries."

CHAPTER SIXTEEN

Somehow, Brigham figured out how to place a massive order of steel beams using Burakgazi's limitless credit card. He was having them delivered to what he jokingly referred to as "the battle zone." Halsey didn't ask for specific details, but she figured it was safe to assume they'd have a few more days to come up with a more specific action plan before their odd supply order was delivered and ready for use.

It took less than twenty-four hours.

On their second morning in the penthouse, Brigham practically jumped with excitement when he got the call confirming the delivery. Halsey had never seen her cousin stuff his face with more food in such a short amount of time after that.

"Hey, feel free to slow down a little," she told him as she finished lacing her boots. "Won't help us much if you choke on your breakfast before we can choke a chimera with a bunch of molten metal."

Brigham made several quick rounds along the edge of

the dining room table, alternating between cramming food into his mouth and collecting the crude but effective maps and attack strategies they'd drawn out the day before. "You should eat *more*, Hal."

"I already ate. I'm full."

"It's not about being hungry." He stopped to finish off a glass of milk, then tapped the stack of papers between his hands on the table to straighten them into a neat pile. "It's about loading up on calories. That's what you really want."

"Yeah, I don't think so…"

He stopped his urgent face-stuffing and regarded his cousin with wide eyes before laughing through a mouthful of food. "Well, we're not getting room service all the way out in the battle zone, even *with* the limitless-credit-card-concierge stuff Burakgazi's got going on. Trust me, I checked."

"So bring some with you in the car."

"Duh. That's what *that* is." He pointed at yet another incoming package beside the front door with the rest of their gathered gear.

Halsey finished tying her boots, straightened, and glanced at the to-go food. "That looks like a giant Happy Meal."

"You'll be happy when you have a meal out there, too. You're welcome." He crammed another handful of salami slices into his mouth, wiped his hands and face with a napkin, then turned from the table so they could start loading up into the rental. "Last chance, Hal. If I were you, I'd stuff in as much as possible."

"Why?"

Brigham stooped to grab their weapon bags and hauled

them to his shoulders. "I mean, if nothing else, this is gonna be a hell of a workout."

Also delivered within that twenty-four-hour window, though it had been sent to the hotel instead of the battle zone, was their second rental car for the duration of their stay in Turkey. Halsey wasn't aware of this. She expected the valet to pull around with the gray-blue, compact sedan they'd already rented. Instead, he stepped from an enormous black Hummer SUV and brought the keys to her cousin.

"Dude."

Brigham grinned. He drew a wad of bills from his pocket and didn't even count them before handing them over. "Thanks, man. No, we're good. That's all for you." He tossed the keys in his hand and turned his grin on Halsey. "You like?"

"That's not our car."

"It is now."

"Brigham, just because you can charge it all to the limitless card doesn't mean you can pay extra to take someone else's Hummer for a joyride."

"*What?*" Her cousin looked shocked for an instant, then he laughed and headed toward the vehicle. "Okay. I see what's going on here."

"Like me trying to help you not get arrested? Glad you can tell."

He pointed the wireless key fob at the vehicle and unlocked the doors with a quick double-click. "You think it's getting to me."

"I have no idea what you're talking about."

"The money, Hal. The prestige. The influence. The…

freedom." That last word put a self-satisfied smirk on his lips before he opened the Hummer's rear door.

"If you're handing valets huge tips to give you someone else's car, then yeah. I'd say it's getting to you." She stopped a few feet behind the vehicle. After Brigham tossed his gear bags into the back, he turned and held out a hand for hers.

"Nope. I'll wait for *our* car, thanks. I'll even drive it if I have to."

"You know, if this wasn't so hilarious, I'd be offended."

"Brigham, I'm serious. Quit screwing around. Come on."

He shrugged and grabbed the rear door's handle. "You do what you want, cuz. I can tell you right now that dinky little sedan doesn't have absolute, full, *over-extended* insurance coverage for any and all types of body damage in the rental agreement. Including but not limited to scratches, fire damage, exploding parts, or dings and dents from natural, unnatural, or otherwise unknown causes." With a haughty tilt of his head, he swung the door shut and circled the vehicle toward the driver's seat.

Halsey stood there for a moment to process the ridiculous information he'd given her. "The hell?"

The driver's side door opened and closed. The Hummer wobbled a little under Brigham's weight, then the diesel engine roared to life like there was a mini-monster trapped somewhere inside.

"Shit." Halsey swung her duffel bag back over her shoulder and hurried toward the passenger-side door. The engine rumbled away as she opened it and peered suspiciously up at her cousin. "You got us another rental?"

"Yep."

"And it's *this* car?"

"Yep."

She stepped back, shot him one more dubious sidelong glance, then opened the rear door to sling her gear onto the back seat.

She climbed into the passenger seat beside her cousin. Brigham was already buckled in and raring to go, both hands drumming the top of the steering wheel. The whole time, he smiled in perfect contentment despite the fidgeting.

Halsey buckled herself in, then dropped her head against the headrest and studied his profile. "Why didn't you just *tell* me you put a Hummer rental on the card?"

"I don't know. Guess I figured *you* wouldn't assume the worst."

"I didn't—" She stopped herself because this was an argument she couldn't win. It shouldn't have even been an argument in the first place. Instead, she swallowed the urge to defend her assumptions and told him, "You're right. I'm sorry."

"All good, man." He shot her a quick smile and a wink before shifting the enormous, rumbling vehicle into drive. They didn't take off right away, though. He regarded her with a frown that wavered between concern and amusement. "You really think two days of 'all expenses paid' would turn me into one of those assholes who think they can buy everything on the menu, plus the people who own it?"

"I…didn't think about it, really."

"You know that's not me, though."

"Of course I know that." Halsey met his gaze as the

guilty pit in her stomach widened a little more. "You've been going crazy on the purchases since the moment Burakgazi slapped that card into your hand, and I... I don't know. I guess I assumed it'd get out of control."

"Fair enough, I guess. Though it's not like either one of us is ever hurting for money..."

"No, I know that. But an unlimited amount with no strings attached? That tends to do weird things to people."

"Hmm." Brigham nodded as he studied her face. "So does stress and a hell of a lotta pressure."

They stared at each other. Halsey clasped her hands together in her lap, forcing herself to keep holding his gaze. *He's either generalizing or trying to tell me something specific. I honestly can't tell which one.*

Her cousin's lips flickered into a mischievous smile, and he drummed the steering wheel again. "So let's go kick one of those in the ass today, okay?"

A wave of relief washed over her, and she faced forward with a determined nod. "I vote for stress and pressure."

"Then it's goddamn unanimous."

Despite how bad she felt about assuming limitless money would have her best friend bribing valets and stealing cars, Halsey couldn't hold back a surprised whoop of laughter when Brigham floored the gas, and the Hummer peeled away from the hotel toward the battle zone.

CHAPTER SEVENTEEN

It took them around two hours to get from their hotel to the site in the middle of the Turkish countryside that Burakgazi had roughly mapped out for them. After another twenty minutes of driving the unmarked dirt road that didn't exist on any public map, they finally encountered the massive order of steel beams that had apparently been delivered earlier that morning.

"Burakgazi *has* to have private contractors for this kinda thing," Halsey thought aloud as she leaned forward and peered at the multiple stacks of ten to twelve beams each.

"You mean like us?" Brigham sniggered. "He's probably got a private contractor to wipe his ass."

"Ew." She cleared her throat and shoved the unwanted image from her mind. "I was talking about getting someone to ship commercial-grade building materials all the way out here to the middle of nowhere. You saw the signs back there when we turned off the main road. This is private property."

"Owned and maintained by one Yusuf Burakgazi. Or at least by all the grunts he pays to handle his properties."

"Probably."

Brigham rolled the Hummer to a slow stop as close as he could safely get to the beams, then cut the engine. "You know, as prepared as the dude was to hand over resources and info once we said yes, he forgot to explain *this*. It's just now hitting me."

Halsey unbuckled her seatbelt and paused to wait for the rest of it. "What is?"

"He already had a map of the battle zone laid out and ready to go. He knew exactly where the chimera's gonna be within a certain area. Where it travels, where it nests, where it *doesn't* go. Hell, he gave us a damn perimeter line."

She opened her mouth to deliver an explanation, but none came. "Huh. He *has* been trying to handle this thing on his own for months. And he's been in the trenches with this thing, like attacking it on his own."

"With a little help from his other friends with guns," Brigham added with a chuckle. "Yep. I know what you're sayin', Hal. He can map out the whole area 'cause he's been here and knows the lay of the land. He didn't need boots on the ground to do any of that, though. He owns the whole…what? Two hundred acres."

"Oh." Her cousin's point dawned on her, and she turned to grab the loose stack of battle-plan papers from the back seat. After quickly shuffling through them, she found both the zoomed-in, printed map of the chimera's "stalking grounds" and the printed aerial view showcasing this property in the center and a bit of the outlying landscape. She squinted as she held both sheets of paper toward the windshield, tilted her head, then turned the aerial-view map sideways. "See anything special here?"

"Like the fact that they're exactly the same? Yep. That's what I wondered about." He leaned closer to the maps, then laughed. "Hey, check it out. You finally got your cold, hard proof!"

"Very funny."

"Yeah, well, it was too easy."

"So is being concerned about what we've been given here." She returned both maps to the stack of papers, then held the collection of their physical plans in her lap while she gazed out the windshield. "He did say the perimeter line was non-negotiable, right?"

"For the chimera? Yeah." Brigham scratched his head and scrunched his face in deep contemplation. "Said the thing didn't ever leave the area. He *didn't* say its ring of destruction was specifically the entire property. Like, *exactly*."

"Too bad we didn't ask him the chicken-or-the-egg question when we had the chance."

He slumped in his seat and fixed her with a crooked smile. "I'm so ready to hear you explain to me how the hell that makes sense."

"All right. We'll call Burakgazi's ownership of this property the chicken. The chimera and the untested border of its stomping grounds can be the egg. We have no idea which of them came first."

There was a long pause before her cousin cleared his throat. "I'm still with ya, Hal. Keep going."

"Meaning one of two things. Either Burakgazi bought the property *because* the chimera was already here, whether or not he was aware of it first. There's a chance he felt like snatching up a piece of land that a mythical monster had claimed as its own territory for the thrill of it."

"Definitely seems like something he'd do. For sure."

"*Or...*" Halsey glanced at the aerial map and pursed her lips. "He had the land first, then the chimera happened to pop over the border to start calling this place home. And it stayed."

"Like those wasp traps," Brigham muttered. "Easy to crawl in, but it's hard as hell to find the way back out."

"Right. So, if we're dealing with the egg here instead of the chicken..."

"That means good ol' Yusuf figured out a way to keep the chimera here."

"And failed to mention that detail in his otherwise ridiculously thorough in-person brief." Halsey shrugged. "Assuming we're actually dealing with the egg. At this point, assumptions are all we have."

Her cousin wrinkled his nose in a pained grimace. "I'm officially rooting for the chicken now. The other way around makes it harder to like the guy as much as I did."

"Hey, come on, cuz." Halsey playfully smacked his arm with the back of a hand. "Don't get all pessimistic on me now."

"You know what? You're right. I'll save that for *after* we're severely disappointed. Good call."

The cousins chuckled as they climbed from the Hummer and gathered their weapons and gear, including the giant, specially prepared to-go box for their on-the-move meal. They took everything to the stacks of steel beams, ready and waiting to be alchemized.

"Either way, though," Brigham added as he dropped his bags and cases onto the dry, browning grass at his feet. "Chicken or egg, we still get to play with a shit-ton of steel."

"Time to show me what you're made of, cuz." Halsey wiggled her eyebrows in a near-perfect copy of the way *he* did every time he was messing with her.

Brigham scoffed as he held her gaze and raised his right hand before giving it a little flick. The beam resting on top of the closest pile shuddered, then slowly levitated a foot above the others. "Oh, you're on."

It took them slightly under an hour to alchemize every steel beam into a different form of easily transportable metal. Because they'd made a fun competition out of it, neither said a word about how they planned to make that job easier on themselves.

Halsey had transformed her half into a temporarily more compact stack of light, silvery-white sheets. She probably could have dragged it on a cart or a DIY sled if she wanted to. Yet what was the point when an elemental could command metal to float through the air behind them?

Once she had the feathery-light metal in the air, she returned to their gear and slung her weapons bag over her shoulder. "You good, dude?"

Brigham grunted as he finished morphing his last beam into a thinner, lighter piece of a different metal with a distinct, bright silver sheen. His hands shook as he finished the job, then he set the final piece on his own personal stack and sighed. He looked up at her and grinned. "Never better. You ready to go hunt a monster?"

She picked up their cardboard lunchbox by the convenient handle and nodded. "Always."

He didn't say a word about her taking responsibility for their meal, which probably had something to do with his focus on getting his stacks of metal to do what he wanted. At first, he seemed to have trouble bringing his alchemized supplies off the ground by more than two feet. After his weapons kit and additional fun toys were strapped on his back, he was able to concentrate more on the magic required to move a former ton of steel.

The cousins headed down the gentle incline from the top of the hill where they'd parked, and their hike into chimera territory began.

Walking into the middle of nowhere was nothing new for them. After all, most monsters preferred the solitude, peace, and relative quiet of the natural world over the chaos of human civilization. For the creatures that didn't need to interact with humans to sustain themselves, that held completely. The ones that had to dive into a town, village, or occasional city to feed on dreams, drink blood, or consume human flesh—living or dead—did their business and got right back out again, as a general rule.

Except for vampires and the occasional converted forest sprite. Yet sprites were harmless as long as they had space for a garden. Plus, the last time anyone had heard of a vampire causing real trouble, a bunch of Halsey's other cousins had been sent out. They broke up the nest, torched it, and buried the evidence by collapsing the mine in which the bloodsuckers had built their home. Before that, the last vampire hunted and neutralized by an Ambrosius elemental had been somewhere up in the Swedish Alps.

That happened back when the current Council members had still been deep in their militia training.

Halsey couldn't decide whether she was amused or disturbed at the idea. Aiden Ambrosius as a child, sitting behind a desk in the Clan library and dutifully listening to Charlemagne's longwinded lectures about anything that caught the man's fancy. Mostly because the first image that had popped into her head was a young boy's body with her dad's enormous, wildly bearded, scarred face settled on tiny, child-sized shoulders. Complete with the dark-brown, supple, oiled leather eyepatch.

Dad had both his eyes until right before I was born. And the beard obviously wasn't a thing until way after he graduated and became an official operative.

No matter how hard she tried, she couldn't change the mental image. It was hard enough to get it out of her head. Eventually, she sniggered as she marched across the open, rolling terrain while towing the lightweight alchemized metal behind her. Not that the weight of it mattered much when hauling supplies by magic alone.

Of course, levitating and maintaining control over a ton of steel was a hell of a lot easier than, say, raising a skyscraper by its steel frame. When it came down to smaller amounts like what they had with them, it was less about weight and more about maneuverability and balance. Especially after Halsey and Brigham reached a small forest of thick deciduous trees stretching across the width of the property border.

So there was no going around it.

Brigham stopped in front of the tree line, looked over his shoulder at the smaller, lighter, but still clunky collection of metal sheets he'd alchemized, and clicked his tongue. "Should've upgraded to an airdrop. A limitless credit card would've covered the cost…"

Halsey fought back another laugh. "They're only trees, cuz."

"Uh-huh. With branches. And bark. And roots. Looks like some of 'em are sticking up in random places, and I really don't like focusing half my mind on steering metal through trees and the other half on not eating shit."

She snorted, raised a hand, and slightly rotated it. In response, her thin sheets of silvery-white metal turned until their length was perfectly vertical. "Helps if you try to get it a little less…all over the place."

"Pshh." He shot her a dubious frown before turning away from her in mock dismissal. "I've got a nice, neat stack of not-steel sheets, thank you very much."

"I never said you didn't."

"I never said you *said* I didn't."

Halsey stared as Brigham rolled his shoulders, rocked his neck from side to side, then interlaced his fingers and stretched them backward to elicit a quick series of knuckle-cracks. Apparently, he was too focused on preparing to haul their gear through the forest to look at her. Or he didn't want her to see how much he wasn't looking forward to this.

"Let's take a hike." With a curt nod, he put one boot in front of the other and slowly passed through the tree line. "Try to keep up, okay?"

She laughed and decided to give him a thirty-second head start before floating her wafer-thin metal along to weave between the sturdy, twisting tree trunks.

Based on the images Burakgazi had provided, this forest stretched incredibly far from northwest to southeast, but it wasn't all that deep. At an average trek-through-the-woods clip, it might have only taken thirty to forty minutes to pass from one side of the long strip to the other. However, Brigham had not set an average pace. He might have even slowed down after the first third of their path through the trees.

Halsey had to give him credit for not throwing in the towel after the first, second, *and* third time his magically transported metal glanced off a tree trunk or an errant branch. Every time his gear bashed against boughs and bark, the woods echoed with the low, wobbling *clang* of metal and Brigham's not-so-muffled growls of frustration.

More than anything, she wanted to provide her cousin with a few helpful pointers for how to avoid the trees, the noise, and his own frustration. Except dishing out free advice to Brigham Ambrosius was like suspending Halsey from active militia duty for bringing home the truth nobody wanted to hear. Meaning it was unappreciated and unsolicited, and he'd probably end up doing the opposite of what she suggested anyway.

Besides, it would only distract him from maintaining his magical hold on the life force inside the metal. That was not a recipe for improvement.

She continued steadily and silently through the trees, staying about fifteen paces to his left, so she didn't lose sight of him but also didn't get in her way. Her thin metal sheets floated along at a perfectly upright angle beside her, slightly adjusting course here and there beneath the gentle pull of her magic to avoid the same fate as Brigham's supplies.

Her cousin made it through almost half an hour of the frustrating obstacle course before he stopped trying to pretend that he wasn't at the end of his rope or that Halsey hadn't noticed.

The next time his floating metal clanged against one tree, then immediately against another, Brigham stopped and released a long, aggravated sigh that ended in a growl. Fortunately, his floating metal stopped beside him, which seemed to be the easiest part of this leg of their mission. For him, at least.

"This blows."

Halsey paused a few yards away and brought her own gear to a gentle halt ahead of her. She turned toward her cousin and tried to look like she hadn't noticed a thing. "You okay?"

"I mean, I'm alive." He spread his arms, faced her, and shrugged. "Which probably doesn't mean a damn thing at this point. I've been making so much noise that I'd be surprised if the chimera *isn't* waiting to strike the second we step out of the trees."

Halsey pressed her lips together and casually shook her head. "It's really not that bad."

Brigham raised an eyebrow. "Oh, yeah? How many branches have *you* broken off in the last thirty minutes?"

"We can go a little slower if you like."

He scoffed and aimed a twitching wave at his floating metal. "Screw that. We've got an invincible chimera to take care of. I only had to vent for a second. Come on."

With that, he took off through the trees again. He

slowed a bit every minute or two to double-check that he had enough room both ahead and behind to avoid more metal-wood collisions. He wasn't quite as successful as he would've liked. Eventually, he quit trying to check the distances because it distracted him from watching his footing.

"Should've let you carry the whole damn thing," he muttered. "This ain't my jam, Hal. I do fire. Sometimes a nice big rock or two. Hell, put any long-range weapon in my hands, even better. But this *finesse* crap?" Brigham stepped over a pile of broken rocks and grimaced when his floating metal barely missed bashing more trees. "You're way better at this kinda thing. *And* at hacking everything with an axe, apparently."

"You're doing great." It didn't sound as reassuring as she'd hoped, so she quickly added, "I think it's more of a composition thing. You know, weight and density—"

"I know what composition means." Her cousin looked back and forth between their levitating, alchemized stacks. "Apparently, I can't actually *use* it the right way. Seriously. Compared to yours, mine looks like a freakin' five-year-old slapped a couple of pieces of sheet metal together and called it good. How the hell did you get those things so *thin*? Looks like they're made out of air."

Halsey shrugged and looked ahead through the trees. If she met her cousin's gaze, she couldn't guarantee the ability to hide the satisfied superiority creeping into her smile. "I went with the lightest metal, man. Pliable. Maneuverable. Super-easy to pull along physically *or* magically…"

"You're giving me nothing with that, Hal. I already chose the lightest metal." Brigham gestured toward his floating silver sheets, then hissed and jerked his hand aside in an attempt to get a quicker response from the metal. The result was that only a corner of one alchemized sheet clanged against a tree instead of the whole flat surface. "I thought aluminum was supposed to be one of the easy ones."

"Hey, aluminum's a good choice, for sure. And it *is* easy." She shot him a sidelong glance. "Only not as easy as lithium."

"Not as..." When it dawned on him, he dropped his head back to stare at the blue sky peeking between the overhead tree branches and groaned. "The world makes sense now."

"Because of lithium?"

"And me totally forgetting about it, yeah. Damn it." Brigham flapped a hand at her and plowed forward through the trees. "You win. Again."

Halsey chucked, then caught sight of a break in the trees not far ahead that signified the other edge of the woods. With an easy hand-wave, she sent her paper-thin, perfectly straight sheets of pure lithium sailing ahead through the trees like a shimmering silver-white specter. "It's not a competition, dude."

"When it's with you? You're damn right it is."

"Hey, we all have our skills."

"Uh-huh. Next time, you're carrying it all." He jerked his hand forward again like he was pulling a stubborn dog on a leash instead of their secret weapon against the chimera. Hopefully. At least he was laughing about it now, which made Halsey feel better about joining him.

They reached the edge of the forest, metal and all.

Ahead of them lay open, rolling hills, summer-lightened grass, and the foothills of a small mountain range in the distance.

Simply making it out of the woods seemed to do a complete one-eighty for Brigham's mood. He rolled his shoulders back and scanned the view while the floating stacks of aluminum sank to the ground behind him. "Much better."

Halsey frowned as she slipped her weapons bag off her shoulder and dropped the whole thing. "You've been in way worse places than a thin little forest."

"Yeah, well, you know what? Last time I walked through the woods with only one other hunter next to me, I got smashed to pieces against those trees. And spent two weeks in medical. So excuse *me* for getting antsy the first time I do it again."

"My bad." She lifted her hands in concession but couldn't wipe the smile off her face. "It bears mentioning, though... Last time you walked through the woods with only one other hunter, it wasn't *me*. Don't get me wrong. Candace is awesome. She's just—"

"She's just not *you*." He snorted and shook his head. "I know. We all know. *Nobody's* you, Hal. Nobody ever will be. The damned ogres probably wouldn't have kicked the shit outta me if you'd been there instead of her. I get it. It's..." He drew a deep breath, smoothed his hair away from his forehead with both hands, then released a self-conscious chuckle. "Whew. Okay. The moment's over. Let's go kick some chimera—"

A gust of warm summer wind raced along the edge of

the forest from the southeast and buffeted the cousins, making them both stagger sideways in surprise.

Neither one of them would have taken notice if the wind hadn't been immediately followed by an enormous shadow rippling across the landscape to blot out the sun.

CHAPTER EIGHTEEN

Instinct, training, and self-preservation immediately took over. Halsey dropped into a crouch to avoid what her brain told her was heading her way. Beside her, Brigham did the same with a small grunt of effort. His reflexes had been right on time, but his rational mind hadn't caught up to reality yet.

Mostly because the reality he'd expected had completely changed.

"Shit," he muttered, steadying himself as the last of the huge shadow rushed over them and the warm sunshine returned. "See, Hal? We totally could've gotten a private airdrop delivery for the steel. A truck driver might not wanna freight everything all the way out here, but it's obviously no big deal for a couple of pilots to—"

"Brigham." Still crouching, Halsey was the only one who'd actually looked up at the source of the enormous shadow. Now she couldn't stop staring at the equally enormous mass soaring above the treetops and ascending at a shallow angle.

Her cousin surveyed her with a frown. "What's wrong with you?"

"I don't think that was an aircraft."

"Ha. Yeah. Because Turkey's known for its giant fucking birds, right?" A bitter laugh escaped him as he shook his head and straightened. "Nice try, cuz. If you wanted someone *that* gullible, you picked the wrong partner for the job, 'cause I'm—"

"Stop talking," she snapped, still staring at the dark shape in the distance that looked a hell of a lot like it was banking back around.

Brigham whirled toward her and spread his arms. "What's your problem?"

"You mean *our* problem?" She pulled her gaze from the thing in the sky, then looked her cousin in the eye so he could see how serious she was and pointed toward the shape.

"What…" Brigham's smile disappeared. He jerked his head in the direction she'd pointed, and his eyes widened as his jaw dropped. "Is that…"

"Yep."

"With…wings?"

"Looks like it, yeah."

"Shit." The only expression she could accurately detect on his face was pure anger. "How the fuck does a chimera have wings?"

"My best guess?" Halsey released a sharp, humorless laugh. Reacting in any other way would've been completely useless. "It got a fun new upgrade somewhere between the last time Burakgazi saw it and…now."

"*What?*" Brigham's face scrunched in disbelief, denial,

and skepticism as he tried to process that. "Then we *are* talking about some kinda evolution here."

"The kind that comes from the Mother of Monsters being out of the box and back on dry land, yeah. Probably."

"Great. So the unkillable monster that could only be defeated by a Greek hero and a *Pegasus* sprouted wings overnight. Now we're standing here like a couple of morons who don't have a single advantage. At all."

"We still have magic." It was supposed to be a reassuring comment, but even Halsey thought it sounded flat and empty. "That's gotta count for something."

"Yeah, as a perfect excuse to get the hell outta here."

She raised an eyebrow in disapproval.

Brigham growled a sigh and rolled his eyes. "Fine. If we die, I'm gonna kill you."

"If we die, I won't try to stop you."

"Good." He glared across the open landscape at the dark speck in the sky that was their target. Gritting his teeth, he reached back and flicked his hand. His stack of alchemized aluminum sheets shuddered, clanged together, then rose off the ground and floated toward him. "Chimera with wings. Proof that nightmares really do come true."

"That's your nightmare?"

"Well, it is *now*."

He looked so certain of that statement without actually seeming scared that Halsey couldn't help but laugh. Her cousin glared at her, but she'd cracked the surface of his aggravation. He shot her a crooked smile. "It gets better and better, doesn't it?"

"Isn't that why we signed up for this gig?"

"You wish."

Despite their new, shocking discovery soaring through the sky and their astronomically diminished chances of success, the young elementals sniggered and focused on their cache of available metal and what they *could* control.

"How much do you think we need to pivot on our Plan A?" Brigham asked as the aluminum pieces shimmered, rippled, and started to thicken and elongate while their bright silver sheen darkened.

Halsey watched her lithium morph under the call of her magic until the entire stack had melted into an amorphous blob of silver without any identifying structure. "Probably not that much."

"Probably. I like the confidence, cuz. Nice."

"Well, we were already gonna start by drawing the thing out of…wherever it happened to be. That hasn't changed. We'll only be aiming more up instead of, you know, directly in front of us."

"Assuming the thing stays in range."

Halsey's magic thrummed and pulsed inside her as she maintained her grasp on the life force inside the shimmering, molten mass that didn't require any heat with an Ambrosius behind the wheel. "If the chimera's out of our magical range, we're out of its attack radius. I'm not too worried about that part."

Brigham stared at his cousin's hovering blob of metal, which wouldn't take on an actual form or even a specific *type* of metal until Halsey decided what to do with it. At least he'd managed to emulate her move with his own half of their battle strategy, which was losing its potential for success by the second.

He cleared his throat. "What *are* you worried about?"

Halsey looked away from her metal and met her cousin's gaze. "Let's go shoot the bastard down."

"Yeah, sure. As soon as you answer the question."

She couldn't. If she took the time to lay out everything that could and probably would go wrong in their attempt, the chimera was likely to swoop down on them and burn them to a crisp before she finished. There was no point in dwelling on all the things that concerned her, anyway. She readjusted the strap of her weapons bag over her shoulder and walked into the open field ahead of the woods.

"Hal. Seriously." Brigham shot a wary glance at the speck in the sky, which now soared almost due east and didn't seem to be coming their way yet. He clenched his jaw and leapt after his cousin. "Not answering a question like that *really* isn't a great way to start off the show, if you know what I mean. Hey."

She stopped to study the chimera's apparent flight path. The simple fact that it *had* a flight path should've been impossible. Yet here they were, standing in an open field and staring at an indestructible, three-headed, fire-breathing monster with *wings*. When her cousin caught up to her and wouldn't quit staring instead of focusing on their target, she muttered, "Everything, Brigham."

"There. Was that so hard to say out loud?"

Halsey smirked. "A little, yeah. Kinda seems pointless, don't you think?"

He shrugged and watched the chimera wheeling through the sky. "I only wanna make sure we're on the same page."

"Great." She tilted her head at the shape. "I don't think it saw us."

"It literally flew right over our heads."

"Yep. Without making a sound or attacking. After everything Burakgazi's put that thing through, I'm sure it's built up an association between people and fighting for its life."

"Maybe it can tell we're not Burakgazi." Brigham cleared his throat. "That's possible, right?"

"Not likely. Unless you've figured out a way to look and smell like something that *isn't* human." Halsey cast him a raised eyebrow, and her cousin rolled his eyes. "Didn't think so. Now, we need to catch its attention."

He grimaced and studied the mass of metal hovering in front of her outstretched hand. "Right. That's only slightly better than waiting here to be dive-bombed or chasing it around the property and hoping it notices."

"Oh, come on, cuz." She smiled crookedly. "This isn't the first time you've gone after something with wings. What about those wyverns?"

"Those things were, like, twenty times smaller than *this*. And so we're clear, this is the first time either of us has gone after something that isn't *supposed* to have wings. There's a big difference."

"You're right." When he looked at her in surprise, it took effort not to laugh at his baffled expression. "Got it all out of your system now?"

Brigham stared at her, then heaved a breath. "Yep. Thanks."

"No problem."

The chimera's dark silhouette banked to the southeast, which only further supported Halsey's theory that the thing was circling the property, AKA its own private hunting grounds. Either as a perimeter check or looking for food. She hoped it was the latter because that would mean the chimera was only operating on basic instincts.

If it's doing a perimeter check, it knows the edges of the property. Which means it's a lot smarter than anyone's probably ever given a chimera credit for. A super-smart chimera isn't gonna make this any easier.

"Okay." Brigham rubbed his hands together and looked pleased with himself when his own floating, molten mass didn't fall to the ground in front of him. "How to catch its attention…"

As if the chimera could hear them, an enormous plume of flame erupted from the black speck. It shot forward in a blazing column like the creature was attacking something in the air.

"Looks more like a dragon," Halsey mused. "Which sends some seriously mixed messages, if you ask—"

"I'm on it." Grinning, Brigham shoved a hand into his pocket and produced one of his silver Zippo lighters with the flipping lid. The sides on this one looked coated in mother-of-pearl panels. Knowing Brigham and his extensive lighter collection, that wasn't far beyond the realm of possibility.

Halsey shrugged and eyed the lighter as he flicked it open in his left hand. "It's gotta be big."

He scoffed and shook his head, not once taking his eyes from the wheeling chimera in the sky. "Please."

"Make sure it goes high enough—"

"Hal." Brigham sparked the lighter into flame, then turned to meet his cousin's gaze. "You gonna let me do my thing, or what?"

"It's been a while since your last official mission. That's all."

"I had a purple face and a few cracked ribs, cuz. Not brain damage."

"That we know of…"

"Yeah, yeah. Keep talkin' shit." He smirked, returned his attention to the chimera, and raised the lighter in front of him. The decent-sized flame flickering at the top didn't seem capable of igniting the kind of blaze they needed to get the chimera's attention. For most elementals, that would've been a tall order.

Yet this was Brigham Ambrosius. Despite all his other quirks, fire was definitely his thing.

The chimera released another bursting column of flame way up in the sky, and Halsey's cousin grinned.

"Well, hello to you, too."

Then he let his magic run wild.

The flame leapt off the lighter and into Brigham's right hand, where it instantly erupted into a massive pillar of fire streaking into the sky. His left hand steadily held the lighter, which kept fueling the flames as he made them bigger and brighter, forcing them up at least a hundred feet.

Halsey chuckled and took a few steps away from her cousin to avoid the insane discomfort of standing so close to an enormous magical fire.

However, Brigham didn't even seem to notice the heat. Which was probably what made him so well-suited to his own personal flame specialty. He only grinned wider.

He let the fiery signal continue for a full ten seconds before lowering both hands and flicking the silver lighter's lid shut with a satisfying *clang*. The flames took longer to peter out on their own, leaving behind the scent of burning fuel, a few wisps of smoke, and a couple of additional degrees added to the already warm August day.

The cousins watched the chimera in silence.

There was no screech or monstrous roar, no burst of flame from the goat-head in reply. It didn't seem like they'd caught the thing's attention at all.

"Huh." Halsey frowned across the field.

"Okay, no." Brigham spread his arms. "There's no way the chimera didn't see that. I mean, that was a hell of a head-turning display."

"Sure was."

"Thanks. So what gives with our monster, huh?"

She shook her head and slowly replied, "I have no idea. Maybe you should try again."

Her cousin laughed bitterly. "You wanna spend the whole day here blasting flames into the sky for no reason? I only have so much lighter fluid."

"You didn't bring any backups?"

"What? *Of course* I brought backups. Come on." He faced the speck in the sky, not really paying attention to it as he gestured in the chimera's direction. "If *that* didn't grab the thing's attention, I don't know what will. That was, like, top power. If we had a fighter jet or something, that'd be a different story. Yet we don't have one, and that's not an option even with Burakgazi's card. I'm pretty sure we couldn't pay even the most insane pilot with a legit death wish to fly out here and engage that thing in—"

"Brigham."

"Lemme at least finish my thought. Damn."

Halsey glanced at her cousin and immediately returned her gaze to the black speck. Now it looked like the chimera was hanging in place, suspended in the air with no movement in any direction. That wasn't a good sign.

"What was my thought?" Brigham gritted his teeth in aggravation, then shook his head. "Whatever. The point I'm trying to make is—"

"Forget your point, dude. Start making a spear. Or… harpoon, or whatever."

"Well, that's just rude. Plus, we can't throw anything at the chimera when it's *that* far away."

Halsey doubled down on her concentration around the molten metal, using her magic to shape the thing into a long, enormous, glimmering weapon. "It's not gonna be that far away for much longer."

"What are you *talking* about?" He gaped at her, and she finally lost her patience.

"Don't look at *me*, Brigham. Get your shit ready to go."

"Hey, what crawled up your—"

"It sees us!"

"What?" Brigham spun to face the rest of the field and the dark speck in the air.

Only it wasn't a dark speck anymore. It was a blot against the blue backdrop of the sky. It only looked like it had been hovering in the same spot because the chimera had banked to face them head-on, its shape unchanging but its size growing by the second.

His eyes widened, and he reached out with both hands toward his own of melted metal that would hopefully be their ticket out of this mess. "Shit."

CHAPTER NINETEEN

By the time the chimera closed half the distance between them, Halsey had shaped her metal into something that looked mostly like a spear. If a *giant* had been there to pick it up in one massive hand, aim at the winged beast, and use it for target practice.

I don't need a giant hand. Only a firm hold on the magic in this weapon and really good aim.

Her aim had been almost perfect since the moment she'd learned how to throw any type of weapon. Continuing that near-perfect streak wouldn't be hard, even against a monster that had sprouted wings without telling anybody its plans. The thing's size would make it a much easier target the closer it got, as long as she and her cousin managed to avoid the thing's fiery attacks from its grotesque back-goat-head.

That part wasn't what worried her.

What worried her was the fact that Brigham seemed overwhelmed by the situation as he fumbled with his molten metal, struggling to mold it into anything other than a shimmering blob.

"Dude." Halsey pulled her hands away from each other to mimic the shape in which she was successfully crafting her enormous metal spear. "Time to make your weapon."

"I *am* making my weapon."

"Melted splatter isn't a weapon, Brigham!"

"Stop yelling!" He grunted and kept reaching out toward the shuddering blob of metal floating in front of him. His hands started to shake, which only intensified his frustrated and slightly terrified growl. Instead of focusing on the work in front of him, he looked back and forth between the metal mass and the chimera racing toward them through the warm air.

When the creature unleashed a monstrous sound somewhere between a lion's roar and a reptilian screech, Brigham cursed and shoved his magic too forcefully against his metallic supplies. Bursts of liquid metal sprayed from the opposite end of the mass as if it had been dumped into a crucible and was splashing over the sides. He simply couldn't get it to take shape.

He's panicking. Great. I told him to work with massive amounts of metal, and now Brigham Ambrosius is panicking.

"Okay, forget about the metal," she shouted as the last of her enormous spear formed in the air. The thing stretched twelve feet long, six inches in diameter, and ended in one of the sharpest points she'd ever crafted.

Her cousin apparently didn't feel like listening as he fumbled to pull his metal into any kind of shape at all.

"Hey! Did you hear me—"

"I'm not gonna *forget about the metal*, Hal! Gimme a sec."

"We don't *have* a sec! I need you on fire guard."

"On *what?*"

Halsey rolled her eyes and pulled on the enormous spear. It sailed smoothly backward, hovering five feet above the grass as it waited for her to launch it with the full momentum of her body and her magic behind it. "You know what I mean. Drop the steel and focus on making sure we don't get burned to a crisp."

"No, I can do this—"

"I know you can, but we're out of time!"

The chimera hurled another terrifying bellow that ended in an earsplitting screech. It couldn't have been more than half a mile away and coming in fast.

Brigham jolted at the sound. The billowing mass of molten steel dropped to the ground in a steaming, hissing puddle. "Shit!"

"I got it. Handle the fire!"

Apparently, it took twice hearing she wanted him to use his strongest elemental magic for the idea to finally sink in. Only then did he stop trembling and square his shoulders to face the chimera head-on.

Facing this direction, he stood six feet in front of his cousin. Normally, it would have been a defensive position that allowed her more time to work with her part of whatever plan they'd come up with. Right now, it only made him look like a moron for putting himself between Halsey and an enormous, screaming chimera.

At least he knows he can handle the fire part. That's my fault. From here on out, we're sticking to our own strengths and not trying to share 'em.

If it had been anyone else, it wouldn't have mattered

what stance or position Brigham had chosen to hold. A chimera's goat-head fire-blast couldn't be fought off with traditional weapons or defense strategies, and there wasn't exactly a lot of time between the first flames spewing from the creature's mouth and whoever stood against it perishing.

Yet if Yusuf Burakgazi had done a single thing right in his ongoing battle with the chimera, it was calling in two Ambrosius elementals.

Specifically these two.

"Get ready," Brigham shouted over the deafening beat of the chimera's huge, powerful wings. "It's about to get hot."

"As long as it's not melt-your-skin-off hot, cuz. Let's do this."

Halsey couldn't see it from behind her cousin, but as the chimera swooped toward the two human-looking figures encroaching on its territory, Brigham broke into a deviously gleaming grin. "Come on, you impossibly evolving bas—"

The roar of heat and air blasting ahead of the chimera drowned out the rest of his confident challenge as the flames dripping around the goat-head's fanged mouth gave way to a gigantic column of churning fire. It didn't seem half as big as it was until the attack was bearing down on them, and the chimera's next wingbeat only made the conflagration more intense.

With a shout of effort and defiance, Brigham reached up with both hands and took full control of the flames that weren't his. The chimera's attack would have flattened anyone else in a pile of burning flesh and smoke. Halsey's cousin stopped it in its tracks.

A thunderous roar blocked out all other sounds until Halsey's ears started ringing, and she caught a glance of the chimera's flames arcing away from the force of Brigham's magic. The fire glanced away a foot from his outstretched hands, curving the trajectory like a metal bowl curving soundwaves.

Halsey almost turned to shield her face and neck from the searing heat, but she didn't. She couldn't.

Her cousin was doing his job perfectly, and she had to do hers. That required open eyes, keen vision, and perfect aim.

The chimera sailed over them, still spraying fire from the goat-head nestled between the lion's shoulder blades.

Gritting her teeth, Halsey hauled her massive iron spear across her body, out, and up. Directly toward the chimera's exposed underbelly.

The iron winked briefly in the firelight. The weapon sailed up with incredible force and speed, fueled by the momentum of her magic and every ounce of strength she possessed. Then the blaze of the chimera's flames drowned out everything else, and she couldn't see what happened after that.

The beast's mighty wings beat furiously, sending gales of dirt and shredded grass up from the ground. Halsey had to turn away and shield her eyes because a dirt-blinded elemental was as useless against this monster as a normie trying to fight it with military-grade weapons.

She thought she heard another roar from the thing's foremost mouth, the lion's head. She couldn't be sure because the howl of fire and wind, along with the rush of her own pulse, pounded in her ears without leaving room for anything else.

Another powerful gust of wind sent her staggering sideways. Then the intensity of heat she'd felt bearing down on her head was suddenly gone, leaving an empty, itching burn across her skin like an afterthought.

Halsey fought to catch her breath and her footing as the debris started to settle. She quickly straightened and turned toward her cousin.

Brigham hadn't moved from where he'd chosen to stand down the chimera, but he'd spun to face her. The excitement and adrenaline that always came from hunting a monster like this lit his wide eyes. Tendrils of thick black smoke curled through the air around him and above his head. Halsey looked for burns on him until she realized the smoke was coming from an enormous ring of charred earth on the valley floor.

The Ambrosius cousins were standing in the middle of it.

"Holy shit." The words puffed breathlessly from Brigham, and he raised a hand to his forehead to shield his eyes from the sun as he scanned the sky. "Did you get it?"

"Of course I got it." She sounded surprisingly confident, even to her own ears, as she started searching for the beast. She hadn't exactly seen her enormous spear hitting their target the way she'd intended, but she couldn't imagine having missed. Halsey didn't miss. "The question is whether or not I got it in the right place."

Brigham snorted. "If you're trying to do this exactly like Bellerophon, we already started out with a few serious improvements. Like the size of that fucking spear, for one."

"Bellerophon hit the chimera in its goat-head mouth with *his* spear," Halsey muttered. "According to the story. Kinda hard to do that from the ground when the thing's flying overhead."

"Yeah, and he had a Pegasus, too. Hate to break it to you, cuz, but if that's what you're looking for, you picked the wrong partner for this particular—"

"Brigham, stop talking." She spoke firmly enough to instantly shut him up. She heard him approach her across the patch of grass that *hadn't* been burned to a crisp, but her focus remained on searching the sky.

When he reached her side, Brigham joined her in the silent search, then whispered, "What now?"

"Well, to start, it'd be nice to find the damn thing. You know, to see whether or not I hit my mark."

"Come on, Hal. Of course you did. You always do."

"I appreciate the vote of confidence, but if that's true, where the hell's the dead chimera?"

That one stumped him.

Together, the cousins searched the open sky, slowly rotating to peer across the expanse of Burakgazi's property, above the tree line spanning the narrow strip of woods, and directly above their heads. There was no sign of the creature that had failed to incinerate them—and that Halsey hopefully hadn't failed to impale.

"That's...weird," Brigham muttered.

"You don't say."

"Come on." When he chuckled in an obvious attempt to lighten the mood, it came out as weak and uncertain as both cousins felt. "It's not like the thing would try to barbeque us before it…up and disappeared."

"It's not like chimeras suddenly sprout wings, either," Halsey muttered, still diligently scanning the skyline. "I wouldn't be so sure of anything right now."

"Goddamn it."

"What?" She turned to face him and found her cousin staring grimly across the valley.

Brigham nodded toward the dark speck in the distance, once more heading toward them at incredible speed. "We can be damn sure that thing isn't dead yet."

Halsey's eyes bulged. "How is that even possible?"

"Maybe you didn't hit it."

"Yeah? When was the last time you saw me miss?"

"I mean, there's a first time for everything—"

"Not for this, Brigham. I didn't *miss*." She hissed and shot her hand out toward the second half of their monster-hunting materials, which at this point was still an amorphous mass of molten metal waiting to be shaped. "Guess it's time for round two."

"Oh. Right. Because someone forgot to write down in the translation that it takes *two* giant fucking spears to bring down a chimera."

"Can you handle this or not?" Now she was shouting at him again, but mostly because she'd split her attention between the conversation and molding the metal. There was no room for worrying whether her tone came across the way she'd wanted.

Brigham stared at her, then whirled to face the oncoming chimera. "You know, out of all the people to ask me such a stupid question, I'm insulted that it's you right now."

"Just focus." The hovering metal elongated as she drew her hands apart, forming a smooth, massive shaft. Then, because the mere thought was an affront to her personal and professional dignity, she couldn't help but mutter, "I didn't miss."

"You know what? Forget I said anything."

"That's a great idea."

"Maybe step back a little this time, so you have a clearer shot." Brigham jerked his head toward the tree line without looking away from the chimera as it thundered another tremendous roar. "I can hold back the flames."

"When it's closer. Can't let that thing split us up." As Halsey completed the second spear she meant to send into the chimera with as much perfect accuracy as the first one, the beast was only a mile away and closing.

"You don't need me to give you a signal or anything, right?"

"What, you mean the deadly flamethrower with wings bearing down on us? *That* signal?"

Brigham snorted. "Sure."

The creature had drawn close enough for the cousins to make out all the gory details, none of which included the protruding end of an enormous spear. There wasn't any gore, either.

What the hell did that thing do to my spear?

"Get ready!" Brigham shouted, raising both hands in preparation for another fiery attack.

Halsey hauled her arms back and the second spear with her. She was as prepared as her cousin to launch another attack. If she had to retreat toward the woods to get it right this time, that was exactly what she'd do.

The chimera bellowed a roar from its gaping lion's mouth as it swooped toward them at top speed with tongues of fire spewing from the goat-head's open mouth.

Then, instead of the flaming fly-by they were expecting, the mythical nightmare threw a wrench in the only real plan they had.

The chimera tucked its wings against its grotesque back and dove toward the ring of charred earth surrounding the elementals. Sprays of dirt, ash, and smoke erupted from the beast's clawed feet as all four of them pounded onto the ground, sending a tremor through the earth beneath the cousins' feet. Its impossible but very real, larger-than-life wings beat twice more to steady the creature's enormous weight on the ground, and the ensuing gust of wind should have made them turn away to shield their eyes.

However, Brigham was quick enough on his feet to send a blast of air away from them to deflect the worst of it, even as he staggered backward across the trembling ground.

The chimera roared again, the sound deafening from up close. Heat and a noxious stench sprayed from its gaping, slathering jaws.

Halsey's stomach leapt into her throat at the overwhelming stink of blood, rotting meat, and death.

As if to accentuate the point that it wasn't here to play, the chimera took a few steps forward, stretching its wings to their fullest expanse, then whipped its tail aside to expose the thing's equally disgusting third head. The serpent's hiss was almost as loud as the lion's roar. The enormous face flickered from side to side, its jaws open wide to expose glistening fangs and blooming beads of legendary venom.

Or maybe that was part of the new and improved version, too.

Time stood still as Halsey and Brigham stared at the beast they'd been contracted to wipe off the face of the planet. Their plan to shoot the thing down while it assaulted them from the sky was now completely useless.

If the cousins had ever been in the habit of needing a Plan B, they probably wouldn't have spent so much time staring at the creature standing eight feet tall and nearly twice as long from nose to tail.

With nothing else to say and no idea what they were supposed to do now, Brigham sighed. "Shit."

"Yep," Halsey murmured, standing perfectly still and trying to keep her eyes on a single chimera head. She chose the lion because it seemed like the "main head" of a creature with more than one. Still, the goat-head dripping flames and the weaving snake head made it hard to stay focused.

He swallowed but didn't lower his hands, so he'd be prepared for a potential fiery attack. His fingers twitched. "So what are we supposed to—"

The chimera cut him off with another earsplitting roar. The lion's voice was understandably the most prevalent, but now that the creature stood this close, Halsey also heard the distinctly human-like scream from the fiery goat-head's mouth above the subtler hiss from the tail-snake. None of those voices on their own would have given her a confidence boost. Heard at the same time, they almost drowned out her ability to think.

Almost.

As the chimera roared, screamed, and snapped powerful serpentine jaws, the monster reared on its hind legs and beat its massive wings for a furious gust of wind. More debris kicked up from the ground, swirling toward and around the cousins as Brigham managed to successfully deflect the minor attacks cast their way. Still, a gust of wind and a few pounds of dirt wasn't anywhere close to the kind of damage this beast could inflict, even on the Ambrosius cousins.

Apparently, the chimera either had no idea it was exposing the softer underside of its belly toward its opponents, or it didn't care.

Rearing up like that was obviously a warning for them to back the hell up and probably get out of the valley altogether. Yet Halsey saw what she'd been looking for, despite having no previous idea what that might have been.

In the center of the chimera's lion-y chest was a darker spot of fur that looked matted with blood. It could've actually been mud or a natural discoloration, but Halsey chose to remain optimistic.

I knew I hit it the first time. The spear probably fell out in flight.

With her confidence renewed, she pulled her arms back one more time to build up the physical momentum she'd let fizzle out with the chimera's surprise landing. Her second alchemized spear drew back with her, ready to meet its target, and Halsey shouted, "Just like that! Keep it upright—"

The chimera roared again, beat its wings, and stomped its forepaws into the earth like it was trying to pound its prey to death beneath massive paws larger than a man's foot and fitted with razor-sharp claws.

"*What?*" Brigham shouted, fighting to keep the debris out of their faces and continue the conversation his cousin had inconveniently started in the middle of a chimera standoff.

"On its back legs! There's a soft spot on its belly. Do whatever you can to get me a good shot!"

"Yeah. Sure. You mean whatever I can to get you a good shot *again*—"

"Brigham!"

"Okay!" He clenched his jaw and braced himself against the last of the chimera's warning blasts of air and hot, reeking breath. He couldn't call on and control two forms of elemental magic at the same time. The shield of air he'd cast around himself and Halsey dropped, and a maelstrom of grass and ashy debris hurtled toward them as Brigham switched to a more offensive tactic.

As the chimera started toward the elementals, Brigham jerked his open hands toward the charred earth between himself and the chimera's glinting front claws. The deafening rumble of dirt and stone obeying the young elemental's command preceded an explosion of earth.

Massive, jagged pillars of deeply buried stone jutted up from beneath the valley floor in quick succession, one after the other. They punched through into fresh air and bright sunlight one by one until the final surge of stone burst up directly beneath the chimera's front paws.

The creature roared, screamed, and hissed, rearing on

its hind legs and desperately beating its wings in an attempt to retreat from the unexpected attack.

For a split second, the monster's reaction surprised Halsey. *Obviously, this thing hasn't gone toe-to-toe with any elementals...*

She forced herself to stop thinking about it because they had a job to do. Now, it was her turn to finish carrying out their ad-hoc plan.

Halsey grunted and flung the razor-tipped spear at what she knew was the same spot on the chimera's underbelly she'd hit the first time, only not hard enough or at close enough range. This time, the spear flew as fast and straight as if she'd loosed it from a giant bow. Her magic's hold on the metal's life force propelled it through the air. Fortunately, the final burst of rock Brigham had drawn up from the earth was slightly off-center from where she stood.

Off-center enough to give her a perfect shot at spearing the chimera in the blood-stained fur on its belly.

Her aim was as true as ever. Halsey was undoubtedly the best shot the Ambrosius Clan had to offer, no matter the weapon.

However, her assessment of the chimera's state and the effectiveness of her current weapon had been grossly overconfident.

The spear struck the dark spot as the monster roared, reared back, and beat its wings. Any other creature would have gone down in an instant. Unfortunately, this wasn't any other creature. It wasn't even any other *chimera*, and now the Ambrosius cousins had a front-row seat to discovering exactly how it was so dangerously different.

And how deeply this thing really was.

The second the spear struck its target in a perfect bulls-eye, a metallic *ping* echoed back. The tip stuck for half a second before the entirety of the enormous weapon splintered and burst into a million glittering silver fragments as if it were made of dry, hollow clay instead.

Halsey froze in place, both hands outstretched toward the chimera in the same position from which she'd loosed her weapon. It was hard to breathe.

No...

"What the fuck!" Brigham screeched.

The chimera spread its wings to their fullest expanse and bellowed at the sky while the goats-head opened its mouth and sprayed a thinner but equally deadly column of dripping flames into the air.

"There go Plans A, B, *and* C. What now?"

CHAPTER TWENTY

Above the chimera's infuriated wailing, Halsey heard her cousin trying to get the situation back under control. She couldn't bring herself to answer him because she hadn't yet regained the ability to speak.

How is that possible? I know I hit it with the first spear. I know that's blood on its fur. The chimera wasn't supposed to be immune to magical attacks, too.

She couldn't bring herself to consider the fact that the Ambrosius Clan's best team of elementals might have failed, let alone the vastly higher likelihood of Halsey and Brigham meeting their untimely and fiery end in the next few minutes. It remained a small, buzzing awareness in the back of her mind because now, they were completely out of options.

"*Hal!*" Brigham roared. "Snap the fuck out of it and talk to me! What do we do now?"

"I..." Halsey sucked in a searing gasp, then blinked against the nauseating stink of the chimera's roaring breath and the intensifying heat as the goat-head finished its warning spray of vertical flames. "Keep it busy."

"That's a hell of a way to kill some time!" He took a step back and almost looked over his shoulder at her before realizing that was probably the last thing anyone should do when facing down a monster like this one. "It'd be a perfect plan if we were trying to *distract* this asshole, but I don't think that's the best—"

The chimera bellowed a startling screech and darted toward the cousins, all three sets of jaws snapping and gnashing as the monster's eyes lit up fiery red.

"Move!" Halsey shouted as she threw herself to one side, and her cousin darted to the other. Pivoting at the end of her narrow escape, she turned toward the chimera and called the life force of the air around her into a roaring vortex of wind. Then she shoved it at the creature's side.

At the same time, Brigham shouted with effort and a little fear, entirely appropriate given the situation, before calling up two more fists of jagged stone.

The chimera staggered sideways under the force of Halsey's stormy blast, which meant the next crushing blow from Brigham's earthen attack cracked against the monster's other side.

Momentarily caught between two magical forces, the chimera's goat-head loosed a bloodcurdling scream and sprayed more flames. This time, they crashed straight into the woods. The closest trees caught fire with several deafening cracks, spraying sparks as an impressive number of branches crashed to the forest floor.

With another deafening bellow, the creature beat its

mighty wings and reared up, trying to both avoid the fire it had created and return its sights to the elementals encroaching on its territory. It was only the luck of the draw that the chimera spun toward Halsey when those enormous front paws crashed down onto the grass that hadn't been incinerated by its first attack.

Halsey reacted on reflex, which had previously been enough to successfully get her through every other monster hunt of her career whenever things went sideways. Today didn't feel like one of those days. Though it was only a temporary solution to the bigger problem of killing an indestructible monster, Halsey reached out to latch onto the life force within the fists of stone Brigham had pulled forth.

Even with smaller boulders and chunks of rock still flying through the air, she had a volley of earthen shards within her grasp. These she sprayed at the snarling chimera. Two of her projectiles bashed the enormous lion's head, eliciting quick grunts of surprise and pain before the creature furiously shook its head. Its mane of thick, shaggy fur seemed particularly suited for keeping the rest of the stony attack at bay, and Halsey could have sworn she saw a handful of those shards disappear *inside* the chimera's mane.

She didn't have a lot of time to reason out what was happening because she was too busy dodging when the flying rocks and stony slivers reversed course and came back toward her.

As if the chimera were deflecting everything with a mighty shake of its head.

Startled by that fun little realization, Halsey dove toward the ground to get her head and chest beneath the debris trajectory. Several stone pieces hurtled over her head with a whistling howl before pelting the grass a few yards behind where she'd slid on her belly, arms outstretched like sliding into home base.

Home base, in this instance, being the ability to continue living instead of getting pummeled to bloody smithereens by her own attack.

If it can do all that with its mane, what the hell can it do if it actually touches one of us?

The answer wasn't forthcoming amid the chaos, but she sure as hell wouldn't lie there on the grass long enough to find out.

"Brigham!" Halsey pushed her chest off the ground and leapt to her feet as the chimera's roar seemed to shake the earth, the trees, and the very air around her. When she spun toward the creature, fervently hoping to find her cousin alive and relatively well on its other side, she was still more focused on calling out her warning than piecing together what she was seeing. "Don't let it touch you!"

There was no sign of Brigham. That probably had to do with the massive conflagration flaring just inside the forest. Halsey staggered backward and lifted both hands to shield her eyes against the glare as the inferno billowed away from the blazing trees and coalesced in the air above the forest.

A giant fist of churning fire pointed downward at the stomping, bellowing, snapping chimera.

Halsey's eyes widened when the combined force of

more fire than she'd ever seen her partner wield at one time bore down on the three-beast hybrid. She had enough time to plant her feet on the ground and brace herself for the ensuing blaze she knew would head toward her at any moment.

So much fire commanded all at once, even with an elemental's magic, didn't simply disappear when it was finished obeying that command. After the flaming fist hit its target and the ground, it had to go *somewhere*.

Her experiential knowledge in the field and a decent understanding of physics made it easy to anticipate the flames crashing onto the valley floor and spreading in all directions with searing heat and incredible force. Halsey prepared to face the oncoming fire with her own magic to make sure she wasn't swallowed up in the process.

Gritting her teeth and forcing herself not to look away, she raised both hands toward the chimera as Brigham's fiery attack struck its target head-on. Literally.

The first flames crashed onto the chimera's goat-head, which unleashed the type of bloodcurdling scream that only terrified children and worked-up goats were capable of. Then a tumbling, swirling, roaring vortex of flame consumed the entire beast.

It only took Halsey three seconds of *not* fighting back the spew of fire with her own magic before she realized that wouldn't be necessary. Instead of splashing around the chimera the way water splashed from a burst water balloon dropped from two stories, the inferno continued swirling around the creature the Ambrosius cousins were so desperate to take down.

Because now it was them or the monster, and Brigham's previous encounter with unnatural ogres months ago was as close to a monster winning the fight as either cousin was willing to get.

Only then did Halsey realize she still hadn't seen or heard from her cousin. Yet *she* wasn't the one keeping all that fire swirling around the chimera, both hiding it from view and drowning out any more of the creature's outraged bellows.

"Brigham!" she shouted over the roar of the flames. She darted around the blaze in an attempt to find her cousin, only half her focus remaining on the idea that at any second now, the chimera might burst through the temporary wall of fire.

Judging by what she'd already seen the monster do, this was probably a temporary distraction and not a foolproof way to bring the creature down.

"*What?*" Brigham called over the noise of the swirling inferno and the gusts of hot air bursting away from it.

"Where are you?" Halsey took a few more steps around the blaze, then ducked when a head-sized fireball escaped and zipped toward her head.

"What did you say?" he shouted again, and she caught a fleeting glimpse of her cousin's jeans and the tips of his sneakers through the roiling air, now thick with smoke and shimmering heat.

"I said don't let it touch you!"

"What do you think I'm trying to *do* here?" The spinning wall of fire shuddered before Brigham doubled down on his magic. "This isn't gonna last forever, Hal!"

"I know."

"A Plan B would really come in handy right about now—"

"Brigham, I *know!*" She stepped away from the heat and looked around, desperately searching for something they could use to their advantage. So far, it seemed like the chimera had *all* the advantages, and the Ambrosius cousins would have to come up with something fast before they ended up like every other military-grade weapon and diligently laid plan Burakgazi had concocted before this.

How the hell are we supposed to stop this thing? All we brought was a bunch of commercial-grade steel, and now that's gone. What else do we have?

It wasn't in her nature to give up when the odds were stacked against her, even odds this great with consequences this deadly. Halsey had gone by the book plenty of times before, but she also hadn't become the Ambrosius Clan's best monster-fighter by always doing what everyone else had done. The last five months alone made that clear.

Come on, Halsey. Think! What haven't we tried yet?

Water was still a potential form of attack, but there was no large source of it in the valley to draw from. Calling the life force of water from every living thing around them would take way too long. Besides, Burakgazi had already scratched drowning and freezing off the list of effective ways to kill this chimera.

They could try to restrain the thing using the strength of the woods. Tree roots, branches, layers of underbrush, maybe a few strangling vines...

That thought was wiped from Halsey's mind when she shot another glance at the edge of the forest past the spinning column of chimera-containing flame. The trees that might have helped them had been set ablaze and were nothing but charred husks and crumbling ash. The rest of the forest was too out of range for either of the cousins' magic to reach.

"Hal?" Brigham called from the other side of the fiery tornado. "Any day now—"

"I'm working on it!" she snapped.

"Okay, well, maybe work a little faster. 'Cause something doesn't feel right..."

She didn't have anywhere near enough time to puzzle out what he meant. What did he feel inside the magic running wild here? What did he mean by "right?" Everything about this job felt so completely *wrong* that it seemed impossible for a clear path to light itself toward their next best move. If there was one.

We're not out of the game yet. We're not dead. Quit thinking like that and focus on an actual solution instead—

The chimera's next almighty roar knocked the rest of her thoughts out of her mind.

The cousins shouldn't have been able to hear that beastly bellow over the chaotic rush of the inferno. They only did because the chimera had managed to thwart them yet again.

There was no reasonable explanation for it, but Halsey found herself staring in horror at the invincible beast's form emerging from the fire. The flames themselves grew smaller, thinner, less violent, and more transparent until she realized the creature was drawing all the fire *into* itself.

No...

She couldn't comprehend a monster that could've burned them to a crisp if they hadn't been on their toes *and* could reabsorb those fires into itself. The thing had overpowered even Brigham's control of the life force within the flames. That had never happened on any of their previous missions, but here was one more first staring them in the face.

That fiery vortex had been their last line of defense, and now it was gone.

So was any extra time Halsey might have had to figure out another attack strategy.

"Hal!" Brigham shouted again, though this time it sounded more like a scream as he struggled to maintain a hold on the flames.

The chimera's snake-headed tail whipped back and forth, hissing and widening its enormous jaws. The lion's head roared again as the creature pawed at the earth, and the goat-head swiveled back and forth, sucking the last of the flames into itself to prepare for a short-lived battle with two elemental monster hunters who were in over their heads.

The goat-head started to glow from the inside out, taking on a red-hot hue like a piece of iron pulled from a forge.

"I can't hold it, Hal!" Brigham grunted against the effort of trying to maintain some kind of control. *"Do something!"*

Halsey wanted to shout back that she was working on it, that she had a plan. Except there was absolutely nothing going through her mind. Not even the thought that this might be the end for both of them because she had nothing left.

Until, at that moment, she felt the stirring buzz of an

altogether different type of magic she hadn't felt to this degree since the day she'd created it.

As the last of the roaring fire disappeared into the goat-head's gaping maw, Halsey spun toward the weapon bag she'd dropped in the grass and the true source of that new magic.

CHAPTER TWENTY-ONE

Halsey's weapon bag was glowing.
Everything else around her seemed to fade.
The copper sphere. It knows what's happening.
She had no idea why she was thinking about the orb like it was a sentient being with wants, feelings, and an awareness of its surroundings, but it felt natural at the moment.
Brigham staggered backward as his magic's hold on the last of the flames snapped. Then he shouted from the other side of the bellowing chimera, "What are you doing?"
"Hoping this works!" She took off running toward her bag but only made a few steps before Brigham shouted for her to watch out, and the chimera's goat-head screamed again.
The next thing she knew, she was being pummeled from behind by a whipping force so strong and powerful that it whisked her off her feet and sent her flying face-first. She heard the spitting hiss of the monster's snake-headed tail behind her left ear, accompanied by a bone-

crushing snap as the serpent's jaws clamped down. Fortunately on nothing but air.

Halsey's chest and stomach hit the ground, knocking the wind from her. She skidded forward across the grass.

"Don't even think about it, asshole!" Brigham shouted at the chimera. "Hey! Over here! Forget *her*. I taste a hell of a lot better!"

Whatever magical attack her cousin launched at the monster, it crackled and rumbled and sent the chimera into another furiously bellowing rage.

Halsey only had a few seconds before the creature took out both of them. If she didn't use those seconds for this last-ditch effort, they had no shot of getting out of here alive.

Gasping for breath, she tried to pick herself up off the grass, but there simply was no time.

"Come on, you motherfucker!" Brigham screamed, egging on the chimera to give his cousin those last few seconds they desperately needed.

Halsey couldn't move fast enough.

She reached out with one hand toward her weapon bag that pulsed with golden light from the inside.

Come on! I need you!

She had no idea how she was going to use the orb or even why the certainty of needing it was so strong.

The why of it didn't matter.

The copper sphere instantly responded to Halsey's call, the way it had responded to her desires days ago in Greta's living room. The force of the response was so powerful that the thing launched through the side of Halsey's duffel bag, ripping the fabric before it zipped through the air toward her outstretched hand.

She didn't have to think about anything after that. Using the orb was as inherent and reflexive as using her own elemental magic, though the feeling of the sphere's magic was nothing like her own.

Halsey rolled off her stomach and onto her side with a bellow of effort and launched the sphere toward the chimera without even having touched the thing. It responded perfectly, whipping past her and darting toward its target as if it had been launched from a giant gun.

The chimera's lion head roared as the creature pounded the earth and spun to face the oncoming threat. The goat-head gave another piercing scream as the fiery glow in its throat flared up with renewed strength. The first spray of flames erupted its open mouth, but there was nothing more after that.

Its unearthly scream cut off abruptly as Halsey's copper orb flew into the goat-head's mouth with a hollow, cracking thump that made her think of a pool ball clunking into the corner pocket of a billiards table.

The goat-head's glowing red eyes widened. The creature choked, its mouth working open and closed in surprise and confusion while thick black smoke spewed from its nostrils. Then the chimera shook its lion head, pawing at the earth and stumbling in a tight circle as the rest of the beast became acutely aware of the magical copper ball stuck in one of its three throats.

What happened next was beyond comprehension.

Halsey felt the presence of the sphere deep inside the goat-head's throat. She didn't tell it what to do because she had no idea how to achieve what she wanted. Yet the orb knew. She felt its understanding and intention even from where she lay in the grass. And it worked on its own to do exactly what its creator wanted.

The chimera stumbled sideways, choking and confused, completely baffled that it had been met with an attack it couldn't handle. The fiery red glow dimmed, replaced by pulsing flashes of bright golden light from Halsey's magical sand sphere. That glow spread through the rest of the monster's body until it encompassed every part of the chimera from within.

Then the entire creature started to *melt*.

At least, that was what it looked like at first. Halsey couldn't move as she stared at the damage being done to the chimera from the inside out.

This is what it would've looked like when Bellerophon hit it with an iron spear. If that had actually happened. Yet this is happening...

The chimera loosed a last few choking growls as it stumbled around, glowing and melting as if it were made of wax.

Brigham staggered back from the oozing chimera. "What the fuck?"

His boot hit a rock, and he didn't even try regaining his balance before he dropped into the grass. He wasn't thinking about tripping, standing, or the jolt of pain that raced up from his tailbone when he landed. He couldn't take his eyes off the grotesque scene before him.

Now it looked like the chimera was being sliced apart like a pat of butter cut by an enormous, invisible knife.

The creature's tail elongated like putty before regaining

its form and density, then dropping to the ground. The moment it hit the grass, it was no longer a serpent-headed tail but an entire serpent, whole and complete.

The goat-head managed one more scream as it stretched its disgusting head toward the sky. It, too, adopted a growing, glowing form, sprouting a back and a belly, four legs, and cloven hooves. It toppled off the lion's back and landed on its side on the ground. The creature bucked and kicked, its legs flailing in all directions. It had no previous knowledge of how to use them.

The lion was the only creature of the chimera's combined three that retained the full use of its body. However, the creature's wings sloughed from its back like dead skin and dropped to the grass with thick thumps. A spray of crimson spurted from the stumps where the wings had been attached to the monster, then they glowed with the orb's magical light and healed in an instant.

It wasn't being sliced apart or bleeding out that ruined the creature's chances. It was the panic, the agony, and the sheer horror of being disassembled by any form of magic, let alone a tiny copper orb, that defeated the chimera.

The serpent thrashed around a moment longer, hissing and spitting, then curled in on itself and lay still.

The goat bucked against the ground, managed to plunge one of its horns deep into the earth, then gave up.

The lion staggered in a slow, bewildered circle, viewing everything through the eyes of a simple wild animal with the mind of what had once been a mythical creature. When it finished its baffled circling, the creature stared at Halsey with surprised golden eyes. It chuffed, pawed weakly at the ground, then tried to take off across the open field to get away from the elemental who had effectively ripped it apart.

After only a few lumbering steps, the lion grunted before collapsing onto the charred grass it had incinerated mere minutes before. Ash and bits of brittle grass puffed away from its massive body to be swept away on the breeze hurtling across the valley.

This would have been enough to shock the Ambrosius cousins into silence for the rest of the day if they'd had the time. However, their frozen shock was interrupted when thin threads of gold and copper light rose from the corpses of the three separate beasts the chimera had become. As if some invisible puppet master were tugging on thousands of tiny strings.

Halsey felt the magic inside those threads as if it was her own, though it definitely wasn't. Still, her hands and arms tingled with the energy of her alchemized copper orb as it drew itself back into its previous form. She hadn't even thought about how the thing would reassemble after using it on an unkillable beast, but the foreign magic apparently knew what to do without any further instruction.

Mere seconds after the last of the dissected chimera's individual beasts hit the ground, never to stir again, the copper orb spun in midair. The last of its glowing filaments settled back into place, then it dropped to the ground with a soft thud.

The sound startled Brigham from his baffled silence as he sat in the grass where he'd fallen, propped on his elbows. "Holy shit."

CHAPTER TWENTY-TWO

Still lying on her side where she'd ducked for cover, Halsey swallowed and tried to respond to her cousin, but her voice wasn't quite working again. She cleared her throat, swallowed again, and managed, "Yeah."

"Did you know it could do that?"

She pushed up into a sitting position so she could shoot her cousin a wide-eyed stare. "I knew it could glow, levitate, and throw itself into my hand. That's it."

The cousins turned their attention back to the animal corpses littering the large swath of chimera-charred grass.

Brigham snorted. "So you threw that psycho ball of magic at our target because...what? It seemed like a fun idea?"

"It came to me, okay?"

"It *came* to you. Hal, you gotta know that sounds—" He stopped himself from saying the one thing most likely to drive his cousin up the wall, but he didn't have to speak it for her to know what he'd been thinking.

"Insane?" Halsey stood and brushed as much of the ash

as she could from her pants and shirt, but it was everywhere. "I know."

He stared at her for a moment longer, not bothering to get off the ground yet. Finally, he huffed a wry laugh and scratched the side of his head. "Well, shit. That was one hell of a Hail Mary."

She spread her arms and tried to smile, but the shock of not being threatened with death, dismemberment, or destruction-by-fire hadn't faded enough for the expression to look real. "I know."

"But how?" Brigham stood as well, trying with an equal lack of success to brush his clothes clean. "How did you *know* throwing that thing at the monster would actually work?"

"I ..." Halsey turned toward the sphere, which sat in the charred grass as innocuously as a tennis ball forgotten after a match. The orb's shiny copper surface glinted in the sun. Of course, now that she wanted answers about how the thing worked and why it was so connected to *her*, it clearly wasn't offering any more help than it already had. "It was glowing. Like it was already aware of what had to be done and needed me to use it. And I didn't know it would do all *that*, but I knew it would work. Somehow. I can't explain it more than that."

"Right." Her cousin eyed the orb, then wrinkled his nose. "Sounds like you know a lot of things you can't explain. I gotta be honest, cuz. It's freaking me the hell out."

"Yeah, that makes two of us."

The Ambrosius cousins stood within the ring of grass unblemished by the chimera's attacks, thanks to Brigham's affinity for the life force of any type of fire. They could only stare at the results of having accomplished this impossible feat.

"That was nuts," Brigham muttered.

"Well, we're alive." Halsey shrugged. "Nothing else matters right now."

He snorted and broke into a wide grin. "*That's* why we're the Ambrosius Clan's best team of hunters. Maybe even the best of all time now. Try to find another team who managed to take down an invincible monster and live to talk about it. I dare you."

Halsey offered him a crooked smile. "You and I both know that's never gonna happen. 'Cause *this* has never happened before."

Brigham sighed and shook his head. "It sure as shit better not happen again. *That* thing…" He pointed at the motionless copper orb. "If I were you, I'd leave that here with the beasts."

Halsey glared at him and reached out with her left hand. The sphere instantly responded. It shot straight into the air, then barreled toward her open palm and hit it with a light smack.

"That thing needs to be locked up, Hal."

"Well, which one is it, *cuz?*" She raised her hand and wiggled the copper orb. "Leave it here or lock it up?"

Now it was Brigham's turn to flash an exasperated glare. "You know what I mean."

"Listen. I'm as weirded out by this thing as you are."

"I seriously doubt that."

Halsey tucked the orb in her jacket pocket and ignored the less-than-enthusiastic commentary. "I can't just *leave* it. Here or anywhere else. We've already got at least *one* normie out there who knows about monsters and has tried everything he can think of to take down a single chimera. The last thing we need is to let him, or anyone else like him, get their hands on something like *this*."

She patted her pocket for emphasis, feeling both reassured and on edge about the orb's solid, rounded weight beneath the canvas fabric.

Her cousin had either stopped paying attention or chose to take the old adage "out of sight, out of mind" to a new level of reality. Instead, he pulled his cell phone from the back pocket of his jeans. "Speaking of that one normie... Shit."

"That's a little harsh, don't you think?" Halsey smirked. "I mean, he did fund our *entire* stay in Turkey."

"Very funny. You know what's not?" Brigham turned his phone toward her. "Falling on my ass and breaking my phone while you broke a chimera."

"Well, at least your phone's still in *one* piece." When he scrunched his face in mock hilarity, she snorted. "Want *me* to call him and share the good news?"

"Go ahead. He was way more impressed with you, anyway."

"Yeah, that's totally what it was." Halsey felt around in her pocket for her phone, which had fortunately survived this mission without a scratch. She pulled up the private number Burakgazi had given them after they'd agreed to take on this unusual job for an even more unusual fee.

Before she had the chance to make the call, her phone rang.

Coming from the same number she'd been about to dial.

She frowned, cleared her throat, and accepted the call. She raised the phone to her ear and plastered on a smile, so she didn't sound as confused as she felt. "Mr. Burakgazi—"

"Congratulations, Halsey," he interrupted, followed by a light, airy chuckle.

"Uh...I'm sorry?"

"Don't be. Congratulations *are* in order, and I simply couldn't wait any longer to offer them."

"Well, thanks." Halsey turned slowly to face her cousin with wide eyes. "Congratulations for what, exactly?"

Burakgazi chuckled again. "Here I was, assuming it was obvious. For being every bit as capable and thorough as I was told you would be. And for still being alive, of course. I must say, that was all very impressive."

"Sorry?"

"Again. Nothing to be sorry *for*. I assure you."

Halsey paused, still staring at Brigham because she couldn't quite allow herself to consider what their first official client's words seemed to imply.

Her cousin spread his arms as he mouthed, "What?"

"Have you been...*watching* us?" she finally asked. "This whole time?"

"Since your vehicle first made it over the property line, yes."

Asking the question had felt ridiculous. Hearing the man admit it without missing a beat was so completely mind-boggling that she couldn't think of anything for a second.

Her expression must have made it clear what Burakgazi's answer had been because Brigham's eyes bulged from his head. Then he muttered, "I had it right. He is totally a shit."

"Was that your partner I heard in the background?"

The man's voice in Halsey's ear ripped her back into business mode enough for her to faintly reply, "Yep."

Apparently, it was plenty to keep their client happy over an insanely strange phone call like this one. "Well, don't let me keep wasting your time, then. Whatever he has to say to me, he can say it over a late lunch. I've sent someone out to collect you."

"To *collect* us?"

"Yes, and I'm looking forward to our next meeting in person, Halsey. We'll see each other soon." With that, the Turkish billionaire, who couldn't have been more than five years older than the Ambrosius cousins, abruptly hung up and left Halsey standing in complete bafflement with the phone still pressed to her ear.

After a sufficient amount of time had passed for the conversation to be over, Brigham slung the strap of his weapon bag over one shoulder and headed toward her. "What did he say? I mean, besides everything that confused you so much you had to repeat it out loud."

"Late lunch," she murmured flatly.

"Huh?"

"You can say whatever you want to his face over a late lunch." She cleared her throat again, slipped the phone back into her pocket, and pressed her lips together. "I guess that was our invitation."

"Awesome." Brigham rolled his eyes. "So...what? The rich dude with swanky hair is gonna fetch us from the hotel for a celebratory 'we're not dead, so he actually has to cough up half a million' lunch?"

"I mean, I guess…"

Neither one of them predicted what Burakgazi actually meant by "sending someone to fetch them." It quickly became apparent when a new sound crested over the whistle of the wind.

Halsey was already on her way toward her own weapon bag, which now boasted a large and inconvenient hole where her copper orb had ripped through, but she stopped when the sound grew too loud to ignore. "Whoa. Hold on a second."

I swear, if there's something else with wings up there that isn't supposed to be, I don't care how much money the guy wants to pay us…

She looked up to scan the blue sky. It was empty except for a handful of stray, puffy clouds floating their way across the mountain peaks at the other end of the valley. Then the rhythmic noise solidified into something that couldn't have belonged to any living creature. Natural, monstrous, or otherwise.

Brigham gazed at the sky as well, but he wore a crooked smile as he clicked his tongue.

Halsey blinked. "Is that…"

"A chopper? Music to my ears, Hal."

A violent gust of air barreled over the treetops before the helicopter surged overhead from the same direction. It shot past the cousins a safe distance beyond the dead beasts lying in the grass before it evened out and lowered to the ground. Dirt, ash, and grass sprayed beneath the swirling surge of the propellers, and Halsey could barely hear herself think.

However, she could hear her cousin shouting at her.

"A *private* fucking chopper!" He grinned, nodded toward the aircraft, and took off without waiting for her to say anything or even look ready to leave.

Of course it is.

She hunkered over her weapon bag. She had to haul it sideways with both hands to avoid letting anything slide out through the giant hole that had saved their lives.

CHAPTER TWENTY-THREE

"Welcome! Welcome." Yusuf Burakgazi grinned and spread his arms wide as Halsey and Brigham were led into the grand dining room inside the man's lavish Turkish estate. "Please. Come join me. Lunch is served, and I believe we still have a few more details to discuss."

The cousins entered slowly, still weary from their near-death experience, and the shock of having defeated the chimera with Halsey's last-minute tactic she hadn't even known would work. Two of their host's massive guards had silently escorted them through Burakgazi's enormous million-dollar home to the vast luncheon spread out on the long dining table that could have fed several dozen but was apparently only meant for three.

"Holy crap," Brigham muttered as he took in the sight of all the food. "He calls this *lunch?*"

"I call it another show of power," Halsey retorted from the side of her mouth. The food didn't interest her. Even if she hadn't almost gotten them both killed out there in that valley, she wouldn't have been able to eat. Something about this entire situation still didn't sit right with her, and she had no idea what.

"Come," Burakgazi prompted again, smiling and nodding like they were here for a party and not the end of their business transaction. "Join me. By the looks of it, I can only imagine how much of an appetite you've worked up today."

When they reached the table, the cousins both pulled out two available chairs to join their host. Halsey sat stiffly in hers and watched their client's face.

Brigham plopped down and practically drooled over the feast in front of him. "This is insane."

"You're welcome to it. Please. Anything you like. It's all here for you."

That was all Brigham needed before he grabbed the plate in front of him and started piling something from every dish onto it.

Burakgazi seemed amused by the sight, but when he turned his gaze to Halsey, his smile faded. He gestured at the food one more time. "Halsey. Please."

"I'm not hungry, but thank you." She tried not to sound petulant because it was the truth. Without having time to settle down after an epic battle with an unkillable beast, maybe it was all the pomp and circumstance and the *smiling* that rubbed her the wrong way.

No. He had cameras all over that valley. He was watching us the whole time. Like this was some kind of game for him.

Whether or not the man picked up on her inherent prickliness, his smile returned as he waved off her comment. "Some water, then. At the least, you must be thirsty. A body needs *something* after an exhibition like yours this afternoon."

Exhibition? Are you fucking kidding me?

"You mean the monster hunt," she corrected firmly. This time, the disapproval in her voice was unmistakable.

Burakgazi offered a small, polite chuckle as he poured her a tall glass of water from a silver pitcher. "Of course. I apologize for the misnomer, Halsey. I was here in my home, watching from within the safety of these walls while you and your partner were out there doing the real work. Do excuse the hastiness of my excitement. I've been looking forward to this moment for quite some time."

With that overdone apology, he handed over the glass of water and dipped his head.

Part of her wanted to decline even the water, but she couldn't deny that she *was* thirsty. She took the offered glass with a quiet, "Thank you."

"You're quite welcome." After a brief glance in Brigham's direction and the sounds of grunting, chewing, swallowing, and finger-licking from his place at the table, Burakgazi paused a moment before diving into the conversation he was so eager to continue. "Now, I'm well aware that your methods for…neutralizing such a threat as the chimera are not entirely public or well-known. At least for the majority of the population, anyway."

Great. Halsey sipped the cold, crisp, slightly sweet water in her glass. *Now he's gonna ask us how magic works.*

"I must admit, while I was viewing your *hunt*—" He shot her a pointed look. "I saw a number of breathtaking maneuvers from beginning to end. The Ambrosius Clan certainly has my respect and recognition. Which isn't entirely useless, I must point out."

"Thanks, man," Brigham muttered as he kept cramming food into his face. He did pause to shoot Burakgazi a grateful look. "We appreciate that."

"But?" Halsey interjected.

Their host fixed his dark-eyed gaze on her, and his smile twitched. "But there's one small detail I can't seem to wrap my head around. I was hoping the two of you would be so kind as to oblige me by answering the question I could not on my own."

"Sure." Brigham grabbed the cloth napkin beside his plate and hastily wiped his mouth. He guzzled the glass of water that had been poured for him, then turned toward their Turkish host. "What's up?"

"The final execution of your hunt, as it were." Burakgazi reached toward one of his staff headed his way with a silver tray and multiple glasses of the Turkish liqueur he'd served at their last meeting. This time, he grabbed a single glass for himself without offering any to his guests. He lifted the delicate cup to his lips but paused to continue his query. "Needless to say, I have access to some of the most advanced surveillance technology. I'm sure I can assume both of you are aware of this. And I was assured several times by several different specialists that all this technology was and is perfectly functional."

The man looked between the cousins, clearly waiting for either of them to accurately predict his unasked question and pipe up with the answer.

If he wants to know something, he should ask it outright. I hate playing these mystery games with my own family. There's no way I'm doing it with a Turkish billionaire.

Halsey raised her eyebrows. "Good to know everything's working the way it's supposed to, then."

Brigham chuckled, then shrugged and went back to downing as much of the feast as he could before he exploded.

Burakgazi sipped his amber liqueur, holding Halsey's gaze the entire time. "Yes, I was glad to hear that myself. The lack of malfunctioning technology does beg the question as to how you actually managed to defeat that creature."

The cousins froze, each perfectly aware now of what their client was asking and what kind of mess they'd gotten themselves into now that they knew they'd been watched through an extensive surveillance system.

Well, now I seriously hope he didn't decide to record *the whole thing for posterity.*

Halsey lowered her glass to the table.

Brigham swallowed noisily, then cleared his throat. "How do you mean?"

"Well, to put it plainly, I had a fantastic view of everything else." Their host sipped his liqueur again. "The fluid metal you two wielded. The manipulation of fire. And the spear-throwing." He nodded at Halsey. "Very impressive."

She held his gaze and said nothing.

"While I'm certain those various methods of yours, no doubt unique to your Clan, would have worked perfectly on different targets, they clearly did not suffice with the chimera. Until your final execution at the end."

"That's usually how battles are finished," she murmured. "At the end."

"Quite." Burakgazi chuckled, then set his glass down and leaned forward. "This particular *deadly blow* of yours, if you will, remains a mystery to me. I don't enjoy mysteries. I prefer to understand the world around me. If I cannot fully understand it, as is admittedly the case with your organization's unique and effective skillset, I wish to at least observe. Which I was quite successful in doing until that final move of yours, Halsey."

"What happened?" Brigham shrugged. "Did you stop watching or something?"

"On the contrary. I was riveted."

Burakgazi didn't take his eyes off Halsey, which gave her the distinct, distasteful feeling that the man might leap from his chair at any second and unleash the beast hidden behind all his money, prestige, and debonair posing.

He continued. "And yet, the only visible action caught on my property's surveillance footage shows Haley reaching toward something before hurling an invisible force at the chimera. Which, against all odds, was the one thing that managed to take the creature down."

Brigham swallowed again and set his fork delicately on his plate. "Oh."

Their host dipped his head. His knowing smile and raised eyebrow lent a feral quality to his outward elegance. "I would very much like to know how you managed to achieve such an outcome."

He wants to know about the orb. Tough break, Yusuf. If normies can't see it, and it doesn't even show up on a state-of-

the-art video feed, I'm not saying a thing about it. Not to you. That wasn't part of our deal.

"Well..." Brigham started, then looked at his cousin.

When she stared back, she knew they'd both been thinking the same thing. Burakgazi couldn't know about the orb, whether or not either of the cousins fully understood why telling him was a bad idea.

With a slight tilt of his head, Brigham wordlessly agreed to keep his mouth shut and offered his mission partner full control of the conversation. Whatever way Halsey preferred to answer such an awkward question from a regular human.

She drew a deep breath and prepared to bullshit the rest of her way through this meeting. "Not everything the Ambrosius Clan is capable of has a logical explanation, Yusuf."

The man's smile twitched again. This time, its biting sting had settled into genuine amusement.

"You're already aware of what our militia has the capability to accomplish every day without the knowledge of the general public." She continued, "I can only assume you're aware of *other* things out there in this world that also defy logic and reason. Like monsters, to be clear."

"Like monsters, yes." Burakgazi tossed back the rest of his liqueur, then grinned at her. "Yet those monsters I *can* see with my own eyes, whether or not they defy reason. With you, Halsey, not everything is as crystal-clear."

"Call it a strategic placement of energetic force, then," she quipped, cocking her head with more attitude than was probably warranted. She wouldn't sit here arguing with a man who could toss out half a million dollars batting an eye, especially after all the millions he'd most likely put into destroying the chimera himself before realizing he didn't have what it took.

"Hmm." Burakgazi shot a glance at Brigham, but Halsey's cousin made it clear he wasn't taking the lead on this conversation. "Is that truly all you're willing to divulge on the subject?"

Halsey nodded. "It is."

"What if I were to offer you—"

"I know you don't like a mystery, Yusuf. Unfortunately, this is one I can't solve for you, and you'll have to accept that." She shrugged, surprised by how much she enjoyed the look of realization and disappointment on the man's face. "Besides, our contract didn't include explaining how Ambrosius magic works. I can't go around spilling militia secrets against my Clan's orders."

The enormous, lavish dining room fell silent. Burakgazi studied Halsey's face, his smile completely gone.

Well, there it is. I won't bow down to answer his questions like everyone else, and I won't take any more of his money to give him what he wants. This is why we shouldn't hunt for hire.

In the sudden tension, Brigham reached toward the platters of food, grabbed a date, and popped it into his mouth.

"You are absolutely correct," their host replied at last. "Please excuse my tendency to pry. Perhaps a little too deeply at times." The man nodded a silent, sophisticated apology that didn't actually include the words "apology" or "I'm sorry." "Your methods are fully your own, whether or not a man like me has the capacity to understand *or* witness them. The point is that you've accomplished more than one seemingly impossible feat today."

Brigham snorted. "That's one way to say it."

Burakgazi ignored the comment. "A successfully completed contract. Fulfilling your obligations both to your organization and to me. And you've managed to surprise me in a way I did not expect. More than once, I might add."

She really wanted to tell the guy off for being so full of himself, and part of her wanted to send him flying across the room for the way he stared at her with a mix of condescension and amusement. Yet she had to continue playing the part. At least until she and her cousin were released from this meeting and could make their way out of Turkey.

She dipped her head and forced a smile. "It's been a productive day."

Their client chuckled. "Indeed." They stared at each other for a moment longer, neither of them willing to give in despite all contractual obligations fulfilled and Yusuf Burakgazi's business with the Ambrosius Clan at an end. "Well, then. If there's nothing else—"

"It's kinda weird, though," Brigham cut in as he stood a few inches from his seat to reach for a piece of baklava.

"What's that?" Burakgazi asked, his smile looking far less genuine now.

Brigham waved the piece of dessert in front of him, twirling his hand in a vague gesture that sent pastry flakes and chopped nuts scattering across the tabletop. "You put all that effort into trying to take that thing down before reaching out to us. For a long time, right? Don't get me wrong. We all know that chimera was one hell of a bastard when it comes to a fight. In the scheme of things, though, it wasn't *that* different from all the other monsters we've fought. It saw a threat, it attacked. After we hit it a few times, the thing retreated to regroup before diving back in."

"Your point?" their host prompted.

"I'm just saying." The young elemental shrugged. "Kinda weird the chimera didn't fly right out of the valley after going through all that trouble. You know, find a different stretch of land that wasn't so…violent."

"That sounds like a question for the professionals, in my opinion."

"Sure, sure. Yeah. Meaning us. I get it." After wiping his mouth with a napkin one more time, Brigham shook his head. "As a professional, I'm saying it's a little weird that thing didn't run a long time ago. Monsters like that are beasts, really. Animals. If their home's threatened and they have no other reason to stay, they'll move on. You know, self-preservation and all that."

Burakgazi dipped his head in consideration. "You said it yourself. That chimera was a wild beast. Who knows why it did anything? I'm merely grateful to have connected with the right professionals who could rid my property of one enormous nuisance I couldn't handle on my own."

"Well, yeah. We did do that…"

"Good. We're all in agreement, then." After sitting back in his chair, the young billionaire crossed one leg over the other and folded his hand in his lap. "Which brings us to our final transaction. I promised to connect you with Halil Aydem once our business was complete. Assuming you were successful in your endeavors, of course. Which you clearly were."

Brigham perked up at the mention of Aydem, the contact for the Order of Skrár that both cousins had separately wanted to contact.

Halsey already had an email address for Aydem, but it was possible that Yusuf Burakgazi could offer something a little more tangible.

Now it's gonna be tricky trying to pretend I've never heard the name before now and didn't try to hold a secret meeting with Aydem in the Grand Bazaar before Brigham caught up to me.

"Sounds good," Brigham replied, trying to be casual about it. "What can you give us, then? An address? Phone number? Email?"

"I can do better than that." Burakgazi stood from his chair, and the Ambrosius cousins followed suit. It seemed like they were about to be led somewhere else in the man's enormous home. He gestured toward the wide arches leading from the dining room into another part of the estate, then took off in that direction. Halsey and Brigham followed, and three pairs of footsteps echoed across the polished marble floors.

"The moment I realized you two had succeeded out there, I made a few calls. If nothing else, I *am* a man of my word," Burakgazi explained as they walked.

He smiled over his shoulder at Halsey, and she couldn't tell if it was only part of his expression or if he'd actually winked at her.

"As it turns out, Mr. Aydem is still in Turkey. I took the liberty of inviting him to my home to arrange a meeting for the three of you to sit down and get to know each other. I hope you don't mind."

Brigham laughed. "Not at all. That's insanely convenient, Yusuf. Thank you."

"It was no problem."

Halsey didn't know how much longer she'd be able to fake a smile. The knot in her stomach had grown even tighter and more nauseating.

Great. He calls in our contact from the Order of Skrár on a whim, and Halil Aydem complies. Doesn't even give me time to tell Brigham I've already tried to meet with the guy. This is gonna be rough.

As they walked down an incredibly wide hallway with numerous arches left open to the warm breeze outside, one of Burakgazi's muscular guards approached and stooped low to mutter in his boss's ear. Burakgazi nodded, then turned toward the Ambrosius cousins without a change in his expression. "Mr. Aydem has arrived on the grounds. He'll be led to you in a moment. Right through there." He gestured toward a set of huge wooden double doors that groaned as two other staff members pulled them open. "Make yourselves at home. If there's anything you need, simply ask for it. It was a pleasure doing business with you both."

When their client extended his hand, Brigham was the first to take it in a firm grasp. "Yes, it was."

The men nodded, smiled, and shook, then Burakgazi turned toward Halsey. He didn't offer a handshake, but he did place a hand on his chest and bow slightly at the hips. "I look forward to seeing you again, Halsey."

"Thanks." It was an awkward reply, but she wouldn't lie and tell him she hoped for the same.

He didn't seem affected by her odd response. Instead, he nodded one more time, added, "If you'll excuse me," then headed across the hallway toward another door that didn't look nearly as grand or opulent as those Halsey and Brigham were expected to enter.

There was a moment of near-weightlessness as the cousins pivoted from one important meeting to something entirely different with Halil Aydem.

Halsey sighed.

This is the only time I'm gonna get to talk to him about all this. I have to at least give him the short version.

She turned toward her cousin and lowered her voice. "Okay, before we go into this other meeting, there's something I need to—"

"Oh, shit, Hal. Look." He smacked the back of his hand against her shoulder as he nodded across the hallway.

She spun to look in the direction he was staring and froze.

Another staff member had preemptively opened the door where Burakgazi had been headed, though the man hadn't quite reached it yet. The cousins had a perfect view of the room on the other side of the door. Spacious, high ceilings, floors covered in expensive rugs, and a collection of tastefully renovated antique furniture.

Those details barely registered, however. Both elementals were too busy staring at the centerpiece of that room. A thick, square pedestal of black marble, its edges coated in lines of gold filigree, rose from the floor in the center of the room. Sitting on the top of the pedestal, propped in a nest of deep-red velvet cushions, was an enormous egg.

The thing couldn't be a prop. Yusuf Burakgazi was clearly not the kind of man who decorated his home with fakes, cheap knockoffs, or copies. No, for their host, only the original would do.

This egg was one such original item the man had employed as quite the conversation piece in whatever room he was entering now. Two and a half feet tall and coated with scales that glinted blazing gold and fiery red, the object was awe-inspiring, to say the least.

Its colors and its undeniable authenticity made Halsey think of the chimera.

This is obscene.

"You're seeing what I'm seeing, right?" Brigham asked.

"Oh, yeah. That's an egg." She nodded, gritting her teeth as they watched Burakgazi approach the open door and nod toward the staff member holding it for him. "Looks a hell of a lot like a *chimera* egg."

Burakgazi entered the room, blocking his treasure from view. He turned back to find both cousins staring at him. His smile widened, and he executed a final bow before the door closed behind him.

"Yeah." Brigham nodded. "Definitely a chimera egg." He turned toward his cousin with wide eyes. "Is that—"

"Why the chimera wouldn't leave this guy alone?" Halsey gritted her teeth, feeling like an idiot for not having all the pieces of the puzzle *before* completing this mission.

"Probably, yeah."

That chimera had an egg. Most likely right there on Burakgazi's property. Her nest. Her home. Then Burakgazi took it for a grand piece of indoor décor, and she couldn't *leave. Not without her egg. Shit, we killed a monster mama trying to protect her young...*

It made her sick to think about it, but they had one more appointment before she could spend any more time or energy working out mysteries of her own. "Come on." She nudged her cousin's shoulder and nodded at the open room where they were supposed to meet Halil Aydem together. "Let's get this done."

CHAPTER TWENTY-FOUR

If Burakgazi had been telling the truth about Aydem having just arrived on the property, he must have put his staff to work getting the man into the room where Halsey and Brigham waited at record speed.

After the doors had closed behind them, Halsey tried to figure out the best way to approach the subject with her cousin. That she hadn't told him the whole truth about her talks with Greta. That she'd already reached out to Halil Aydem once in an attempt to get more information from the Order of Skrár about her magic and the copper orb she'd alchemized. Somehow, starting that conversation with Brigham felt like the hardest part.

She took five minutes to try to piece the right words together as Brigham paced around the room, studying the furniture, cushions, expensive china, and crystal dishes on display. When she finally opened her mouth to start, a smaller door at the other end of the room opened.

Brigham stopped pacing, and Halsey immediately stood.

Finally. We can get some of our questions answered. If we're doing it together, that's even better.

Neither of the cousins had seen a picture of Halil Aydem, nor had they been told what to expect of the man other than he might be willing to clarify a few mysteries they'd discovered in the last few months. The man entering the room looked in his mid-to-late fifties, with a thin gray mustache and a loosely flowing linen shirt.

He was also incredibly familiar. When Halsey finally recognized him as one of the men who'd been sitting in the tea shop during her first attempt to meet with Aydem, she couldn't help the feeling that something wasn't right here.

Unless this guy is actually Halil Aydem, this isn't gonna go well.

Brigham didn't recognize the man at all, which seemed to be a good thing until he plastered a good-natured smile onto his face and stepped forward to meet their guest. "Mr. Aydem. It's a pleasure to finally meet you. My name's—"

"Brigham Caratacus Ambrosius." The mustachioed man nodded and spared Brigham's outstretched hand a glance but did not take it. He turned his gaze to Halsey. "And Halsey Margaret Ambrosius."

"Huh. Sounds like Burakgazi was pretty thorough." Brigham chuckled and slowly lowered his hand, frowning at the odd way their newest contact had presented himself.

The man stared only at Halsey, which made the knot in her stomach tighten and threaten to burst. "Mr. Aydem sends his regards and his sympathies, but he is unable to meet with you at this time."

"What?" Brigham stepped back and frowned. "You're not Halil Aydem?"

The man shot him a look of disdain. "I am not."

"We were told Mr. Aydem was willing to meet with us," Halsey added. "Here in Yusuf Burakgazi's home."

Aydem's messenger scanned the room and calmly replied, "Circumstances have changed."

Brigham snorted. "In ten minutes?"

Halsey couldn't pinpoint why, but this man's calm, apathetic, almost lazy way of speaking to them infuriated her more than she could explain.

If he knows who I am, he knows I tried to meet with Aydem already. Now he's treating the whole thing like a game.

"What circumstances?" she asked firmly.

Their new acquaintance, who hadn't given his name, spun from the painting he'd been studying and looked forth between the cousins' baffled expressions. "Mr. Aydem is not in the habit of providing second chances when the first has been so shamefully squandered."

"Good to know," Brigham cut in. "Now, how about we get our *first* chance?"

"Mr. Aydem will not be speaking with you." This time, the messenger stared at Brigham while he said it, which made the statement sound a whole lot like this contact wanted nothing to do with Brigham specifically.

The young elemental frowned and folded his arms. "I gotta admit that's a little insulting."

When he turned toward Halsey one more time, she lifted her chin and refused to let Aydem's messenger see how put off she was by this sudden change of plans. Even when she'd only been planning to have this meeting for under ten minutes.

"It is recommended that you get your affairs in order

before attempting to contact Mr. Aydem again. Good day." The man whirled toward the smaller door at the opposite end of the room, effectively ending their important meeting before it had begun.

Seriously? I'm getting turned down twice? Whatever this guy's problem is, it's not my fault. I haven't done anything to him.

"Hey, wait a minute," Brigham called, but the messenger didn't stop. He turned toward his cousin and fixed her with a confused frown.

"That's incredibly vague advice," Halsey called across the room before taking off after the nameless man. "Hey! If Mr. Aydem has requirements that need to be met before he sees anyone in person, at least tell us what those are."

"I just have." The man wrapped his sun-darkened hand around the doorknob. "Now, if you'll excuse me—"

"No." Halsey acted on instinct and reached for the life force inside the wooden door as the man started to open it. Her magic overpowered the messenger's arm, and the door slammed shut.

If anyone else had been watching, they would have been more likely to think Yusuf Burakgazi's enormous Turkish estate suffered from a haunting than an angry young elemental who'd had enough.

The messenger reacted by lowering his hand and releasing a heavy sigh.

Halsey pointed at him as she approached. "We need to talk to Halil Aydem. That's why we're here."

"That simply is not possible."

"*Why not?*" she shouted.

He spun to face her, this time wearing an alarmingly tight grin that made him look insane.

"Hal," Brigham murmured as he approached them. "Maybe—"

"No. The Order of Skrár's supposed to be a resource for all things magic and monsters, right? If they're handing out *our* name to someone like Burakgazi, the least they can do is sit down with the elementals they're pimping out for hunting contracts. Why aren't we worth meeting with?"

The man's tight smile remained unchanged. "Because Mr. Aydem knows you are not prepared for the conversation you claim to want."

"How does *he* know what we want? We haven't even had the chance to explain—"

"And would you be capable of explaining what happened with your most recent objective? Of how you managed to rip that beast apart?"

"What the…" Brigham stepped back, thoroughly confused by how quickly information seemed to spread around here.

Halsey glared at the messenger, reached into her jacket, and pulled out the copper orb. "With this. I did it with this."

"Yes." He didn't spare the transmuted magic orb a single glance. "And what, exactly, *is* it?"

Her mouth popped open, and she tried to come up with something that wouldn't make her sound completely ridiculous. That was impossible, so she looked at the sphere and muttered, "I don't know. That's why I want to meet with Mr. Aydem. Why *we* want to meet with him. We have a lot of questions about—"

"One cannot know where one is headed without first

understanding where one has been," he interrupted. "You, Halsey Ambrosius, will not be ready for the truth you seek until you have uncovered the truth you *need*."

"This *is* the truth I need." She shook the orb in her hand. "If anyone knows what this thing is and why it works the way it does for me, it's the Order of Skrár. That's why I want to meet with Mr. Aydem. Plus, there are a lot of weird things going on in the world right now. If the Order has answers, living records, we could *really* use some help with this. Mr. Aydem has to know that, doesn't he?"

The messenger chuckled and dipped his head. "Mr. Aydem is not a history book, Miss Ambrosius. If you wish to dig through the living records of the Order of Skrár, I strongly suggest you dig through the records of your *own* family first. Until then, nothing Mr. Aydem might offer you will be of any use."

Halsey swallowed and fought not to completely lose it on this man who was as skilled at talking in riddles as Greta Ambrosius. "There's nothing in our Clan library that even remotely covers this stuff."

"The truth is rarely captured on parchment or paper. These records are more personal. More…animated."

"I have no idea what you're talking about."

"The living records of your Clan." The man pursed his lips, growing more agitated by the second. "You might consider starting with your Clan matriarch. Good day."

With that, he jerked the door open and wasn't met with any magical Ambrosius resistance this time. Seconds later, the door closed again. Aydem's messenger was gone, and Halsey and Brigham were left alone in the massive room to come to terms with the results.

"Damn," Brigham murmured. "What the hell happened?"

Halsey seethed and glared at the closed door, her fist clenched around the copper orb's cold, hard metallic surface, which felt like it was starting to warm up again.

Meemaw sends me to Halil Aydem without bothering to tell me he's part of the Order. Now the guy's messenger told me to go back to Meemaw for the truth. The truth my family has been hiding from me, but I didn't want to believe they'd actually do something like that.

"Hal." Brigham gently touched her shoulder. "Are you okay?"

"I am so far from okay right now." She forced herself to look her cousin in the eye and tried to ignore the flicker of fear she saw there. "We just got sent on another magical fucking goose chase, and I'm gonna end this."

CHAPTER TWENTY-FIVE

For the first time since officially becoming an Ambrosius Clan operative, Halsey directly and deliberately broke all protocol after returning from a mission. It showed up in the form of commandeering an ATV from the maintenance garage behind her family's enormous estate house and racing it at top speed across the rolling Texas countryside that made up the Ambrosius Clan property.

Brigham barely managed to hop on behind her. If he hadn't, she probably would have left him in the dust.

In the back of her mind, she was vaguely aware that he wasn't holding onto her like he usually did as the ATV rumbled, bounced, and jolted across the semi-rocky terrain.

Most of her focus was on where she was going. What lay in front of her and not behind.

He can be pissed for as long as he needs to, and I'm right there with him. Not all of this is on me, though. I'm not leaving 'til I get some actual answers this time.

Though her cousin had essentially been giving her the

cold shoulder since before they'd left Turkey, he'd stuck with her now that they were home. Brigham wanted answers too. She knew that.

Whether either of them got the answers they *wanted* didn't matter at this point. All that mattered was clearing the sludge of their past and their family's history and figuring out how the hell they'd gotten sucked into the middle of it.

When Halsey took the ATV way too fast over a particularly rough, bumpy patch of terrain, nearly throwing Brigham off, he hissed and clutched her around the middle to keep himself in his seat. He quickly let go of her before shouting, "We're not gonna get there any faster if you kill us."

Halsey gritted her teeth and kept staring ahead as she tightened her grip on the ATV's throttle. If she could've made the thing go any faster at that moment, she would have.

"Hal!"

When he got no reply from her, Brigham growled in frustration and focused on *not* falling off the back of a dangerously speeding four-wheeler instead of trying to reason with his cousin.

Sooner than she'd expected, the vibrant vegetation of the greenbelt running across the property came into view. Then they whizzed past the trees on the right, the rush of the river barely audible over the wind buffeting her ears and whipping her long, dark hair behind her into Brigham's face. He'd given up trying to keep the ends out of his eyes and mouth.

The ATV raced over the last little hill too quickly and

caught more air on the other side than it should have been able to handle.

"What are you—" The four-wheeler crashing onto the grass cut off Brigham's shout. The impact jarred them in the seat and made the vehicle fishtail across the ground.

Halsey didn't let up on the gas.

"You *are* trying to kill us," he muttered angrily. "This is the way it ends, huh? Nice. Good work."

An image of lashing out and shoving him off the side of the ATV flashed through her mind, but she wouldn't act on it. Besides, the front of Greta's little bungalow nestled in the trees beside the river had come into view. Now, that was her only focus.

The ATV didn't slow until they were ten feet from the front porch, and Brigham let out a wordless shout when he thought his cousin would drive them directly through the side of the house.

Halsey jerked the wheel to the left, turning the ATV into a screeching, growling skid as she hit the brakes. It took her two seconds to realize she had successfully stopped the thing before they were in any real danger of crashing. She leapt off the vehicle and marched up the front porch steps.

Amid the groans of the ATV's frame and the low, sputtering rumble of the engine, Brigham stared after her, then rolled his eyes. "Can't even finish the damn…"

He couldn't finish his grumbled sentence, either. He leaned forward to cut off the engine with a quick jerk before swinging a leg over the seat and getting his feet back on solid ground. "Hal!"

The screen door clapped shut behind her, followed by her footsteps stomping toward the front door.

"If you don't want me in there with you, say something," he called after her.

She couldn't say anything. Not even that she *did* want him with her for this. Of course she did. The fact that he was even giving her a choice right now was almost too much to handle, so she said nothing.

That was an answer by itself. With a curt nod his cousin didn't see, Brigham stormed up the front porch steps, swung the door open with a bang, and hurried after her.

Before even thinking to knock, Halsey had already tried the front doorknob with a few quick, furious twists, only to find it locked.

Seriously? Since when does Meemaw lock her front door? Since I found out that she does *have something to hide?*

The next thing she knew, she was pounding on the door with a fist and shouting, "Greta! Open the door!"

She only had to go through one round of commands before a light click came from the doorknob.

The door slowly opened, and Greta Ambrosius' face peeked through the narrow opening to scan her granddaughter. "I *know* you weren't raised to think *that's* how you get invited into someone else's home."

"We need to talk," Halsey growled.

"You'll have to come back another time, kid. I'm a little busy here. Doing...stuff—hey!" Greta stumbled aside when her granddaughter shoved open the front door anyway and barged into the little bungalow. "Well, *excuse* you."

"Hal!" Brigham jumped through the open door and grabbed his grandmother's shoulders. "You okay?"

"Ha. It'll take more than a pissed-off twenty-something to knock *me* over." Greta shut the door again, then turned toward Halsey, who stood in the living room with her arms folded. "And *this* twenty-something's really starting to piss me off."

"You lied to us."

"I'm sorry. *What*, now?" Greta walked tersely into the living room with a confused and unimpressed Brigham following behind her.

"Don't act like you have no idea what I'm talking about, Greta." Using her grandmother's first name was the only way Halsey could think to get across how serious she was. It only made Greta's eyes widen a little, but that was enough of a reaction. "Now, I need to know what you've been keeping from me." Her gaze darted toward Brigham. "From *us*."

Greta scoffed. "Girl, I don't know what happened in Turkey, but maybe you need a little more time to—"

"I'm not tired. I'm not imagining things, and I'm not leaving this house until you tell me what I want to know! All of it!"

"Hal, come on." Brigham spread his arms. "We don't need to—"

"Yes, I do." Halsey nodded. "I *do* need to do this, Brigham. She's been hiding something massive from us for a long time, and it all comes out. Today!"

He turned a sorrowful look on their grandmother and shook his head. "Turkey was weird."

"Yeah, I bet." Greta gave him a reassuring pat and returned her attention to the only grandchild of hers who would dare to barge into her house and start demanding things. Halsey was also probably the one grandchild of hers who deserved exactly what she asked for, even if Greta didn't want a thing to do with it. "I don't know what you want from me, Halsey."

"The truth."

"About what?"

"About *everything!*" Halsey pulled the copper orb from her jacket and angrily shook it in her grandmother's direction. "Starting with why a man from the Order of Skrár told me I had to dig through my family history with *you* before they'd even consider helping me figure out what *this* is. The way he said it made it pretty damn clear you'd know what he meant."

Greta stared at her granddaughter as if she meant to throw the young elemental through the living room window. She inhaled deeply through her nose and released a long sigh. "Our family history is…long. Convoluted. Messy. You get the picture."

"So you thought it was a better idea to keep the truth from me?" Halsey laughed bitterly. "This is why the Council's been against me from the beginning, isn't it? Even since *before* we found that coffin in Ireland. What the hell are they hiding?"

Brigham grimaced at the thought of how frequently the Ambrosius Clan Council had gone out of their way to make his mission partner look and feel like her choices were completely out of line.

A tight smile flickered across Greta's lips. "Maybe this is a conversation better had another time—"

"Maybe you thought you had *more* time to cover your tracks," Halsey countered. "That's over now. We looked like idiots in Turkey, Greta. Like we had no idea who and what we are, and the Order said we weren't *ready* for our answers. Whatever our family did to the Order of Skrár to make them reject us like that, whatever the Council did, we need to know that part of our family history. And *you* need to quit trying to cover it up. So start talking."

The bungalow fell silent, then Greta slowly crossed the room and plopped into her armchair in front of the empty fireplace. After another deep breath, she nodded. "Fine."

"Fine?"

"That's what I said, girl. Take a seat." The woman watched her grandchildren intently, as if they were feral animals who might attack her at any second.

Brigham hurried toward the far end of the couch and dropped onto the cushions.

Halsey took longer, not willing to break away from Greta's gaze, because she knew she was about to get the information she should have had from the beginning.

This isn't gonna be pretty. The truth hardly ever is, right?

When Greta was satisfied that her grandchildren were paying attention, she popped her lips and rubbed the bottom of her chin in thought. "There *are* some things about our family's history you simply haven't been exposed to yet. Honestly, I'm amazed we've gone this long without having this conversation."

"Only took more visits than it should have," Halsey quipped.

Her grandmother cracked a smile. "Somebody's attitude has an attitude today."

"What are we talking about here?" Brigham asked in an attempt to smooth over the tension. "Some deal with the

Order of Skrár? Did the Council piss them off or something? What kind of family history would make people like that not want to help us?"

"Good questions," Greta replied. "I'm afraid it's complicated, though. This is the family history they never taught you in school. Obviously. I can tell you they sure as hell should have." She glanced between her grandchildren with grim determination. "Looks like it's time to change that."

Get sneak peeks, exclusive giveaways, behind the scenes content, and more. PLUS you'll be notified of special **one day only fan pricing** on new releases.

Sign up today to get free stories.

Visit: https://marthacarr.com/read-free-stories/

AUTHOR NOTES - MARTHA CARR
MARCH 7, 2023

Spring is busy springing here in Austin. Sure, sure, it's still snowing and icing over in most of the country, but not here. March heralds in spring here and I make the most of it, knowing full well that summer approaches and 100-plus degree days with it. That's our equivalent to your winter except driving conditions are still good. A big plus.

If you follow me on Facebook you also know I'm an avid gardener. Gardening is particularly good for me because it manages to combine meditation, exercise, patience, humor and determination in something that I love so I'm gonna keep doing it.

All great tools in life that are not one-and-done things. Even great tools to work out a great plot and write a good story.

Spring is also like the gun going off at the start of a race. Even the hint that spring is near starts a lot of preparation. This is where the exercise part really comes in. Removing the dead, assessing the other plants for bugs or illnesses, repairing some irrigation and standing back to look at my tiny landscape portrait to see what I can add or change are all things that happened in the last few months. And it all required a lot of toting, squatting, bending and just muscling things around the yard.

But it's spring! Soil has been turned, compost tea has been added everywhere and new plants have been added.

I never notice how many dips and bumps and sudden turns there are till I'm driving around with twenty gallons of smelly, murky compost tea in the back, wondering if it's sloshing around back there. Three years going and still no spills. May that continue. A spill would mean that can't-quite-place-it-smell would linger in my car forever.

The patience comes in after the winter and a particularly hardy frost that almost killed off a few things. Almost, but not quite. The roots are still alive, which means it'll come back – eventually. That spot in the garden will look bare or like it has sticks growing out of it for at least a few more weeks, maybe a month. Then there's the summer plants that needed to be cut back, and were and won't start really growing for a little while longer. More patience. Gardening in the long term is not about instant gratification or bending anything to my will.

It's about fitting myself to what is, rather than insisting things go my way or else.

Determination, though also plays a part in having a successful garden. By the way, successful in a garden is very subjective. In my case it means a carefully planned out garden looks like something nature did a great job of planning and makes a visitor grow quiet and take deeper breaths. But things don't always go as planned. Things break, plants don't like where they've been planted, mulch gets put down where it doesn't belong, or rain doesn't come or it comes in droves. On some days it can seem overwhelming, much like a difficult plot can in the middle of a book sometimes, and it's a reminder to walk away for at least a day and let it be. It'll still be there tomorrow and the beginning of an answer might be there too. It's okay. Not everything has to be fixed or changed today.

Humor is a requirement in order to remain peaceful and once again, fit myself to what is and appreciate the bigger picture. In my case, I have two large dogs – Bluebell, the elder blue pittie, and Lois Lane, the eighty-pound pointer mix who is the same age but doesn't know it and runs around the garden like a lit rocket. Things are going to get stepped on. Not as much as you'd think, but some. Plus, she has a weird superpower. Lois can smell out a buried rock and will insist on digging it up. It's been useful to get a lot of rocks out of the garden and not useful when the rock is under a plant. Then there's her love of the smell of compost tea and her willingness to eat the plant that has some clinging to it.

In the spring I have to follow Lois everywhere. On top of that, she is deaf – more patience and exercise on my part because I have to run as fast as I can to stop her from getting that plant out of the ground or eating the last leaf, while being okay with whatever has already happened.

It's all good because every day I can add in a little bit of each of the benefits I get out of the garden, I take all of that with me into the rest of my life and everything is just a little easier. Same circumstances, different responses. My focus is on what's working and my attitude is that everything will work out in the end and my life is filled with more gratitude and a kind of ease. May that be true for everyone this season, whenever spring finally finds you.

I'd write more, but there's a garden calling me before I have to get back to working on a certain plot about some dragons. More adventures to follow.

AUTHOR NOTES - MICHAEL ANDERLE

MARCH 7, 2023

Thank you for not only reading this book but these author notes as well!

I have no dogs. There is a reason.

I have to admit I chuckled when I read that Lois Lane would dig up rocks, even if the rocks were under living plants.

Occasionally, I see Martha's dogs on Zoom calls when we are talking stories, business, or just whatever. Lois Lane is not a small dog. So, with size seven paws, I can't imagine she creates dainty holes in Martha's flowerbeds when she decides to de-rock it.

My collaborator has zen patience and a dry sense of humor, so she lets things like a dug-up flowerbed wash over her.

I'm not that way.

Back when I was younger, frankly dumber, and wanted to give our kids options "to experience life," I was emotionally manipulated into approving the acquisition of a puppy (mistake number 2. The first mistake was contemplating getting a large animal in the first place). This puppy came into our life not too long after we moved into our first brand-new home.

You know, the kind of home that has brand-new carpet? I didn't realize that dogs really, really... (insert "really" about twenty more times) like to dig.

You know what dogs can't do? They can't dig through concrete. Know what dogs *can* do? They can dig through a brand-new carpet on the way to the concrete.

I'm still pissed. It's been over twenty years, and I'm *still* pissed. I should let it go. I know. I tell myself the same thing.

I don't own that home. The carpet was destroyed by three boys in a couple of years anyway.

But you should have seen the bare carpet underlayment. And the puppy. The puppy that didn't care that I didn't have the money to fix that carpet, and I *couldn't* do what I wanted.

Which had to do with time manipulation and making different choices in my life.

That particular dog experience (not the last grievance I've got against dogs who have been in my life) is my most troubling.

Note: I've never owned a dog *I* wanted. The dogs have come into my life at the behest of parents, kids, wife, etc. I'm not sure what I would do if I had gone dog dating and had a different attitude about the relationship.

What's Dog Dating?

You know, you go looking for the dog on purpose? You research the dog breeds and what you are looking to get out of the relationship. You are aware of the needs of the dog, and as a responsible adult, you accept the thoughtful exchange of food, walks, cleanup, and destruction for emotional support, wagging tails, and sloppy licks when you are down. You get those after Dog-Marriage (purchase/acquisition/Nazi Background Research done on you before adopt. That stuff.)

Don't get me started on cats.

Watch. After all of these comments, a dog will enter my life in the next week. Joke's on me.

Chat with you in the next book.

Ad Aeternitatem,

Michael Anderle

MORE STORIES with Michael newsletter HERE: https://michael.beehiiv.com/

THE ROGUE REGIMENT

Z Thornbrook and her cousins are like any other Oriceran pixie on Earth. Mischief is their middle name, and for the last hundred and fifty years, that's been their game.

But what happens when a gang of rogue pixies takes the troublemaking just a little too far?

They get noticed. By the U.S. Army. And playtime is over.

Now that they've been caught, it's time for Z, her cousins, and the entire pixie gang to face the music, and they only have two choices. Sign their lives away to enter an experimental new program for magical Army soldiers - or accept a one-way ticket back to Oriceran for good.

For any other pixie, this would be a no-brainer. They don't back down, and they definitely don't take orders from anyone, even other pixies. But for Z and her eccentric cousins, returning to their home planet is a fate worse than death.

It's time to lace up their boots and stand at attention —or not.

Because the Thornbrook pixies are heading off to magical Bootcamp run by humans, and the Army had no idea what they were getting themselves into.

Z, Domino, and Echo must find the acceptable middle ground between being who they are, in all their chaotic pixie glory, and following the terms of their magically binding contract.

But training three Army pixies is no joke—if it's even possible at all.

Can Z and her cousins learn to rein in the chaos as new magical Army recruits, or will they take it too far and be shipped off to Oriceran, where an even darker menace awaits?

Claim your copy today!

BOOKS BY MARTHA CARR

THE LEIRA CHRONICLES
CASE FILES OF AN URBAN WITCH
DIARY OF A DARK MONSTER
THE EVERMORES CHRONICLES
SOUL STONE MAGE
THE KACY CHRONICLES
MIDWEST MAGIC CHRONICLES
THE FAIRHAVEN CHRONICLES
I FEAR NO EVIL
THE DANIEL CODEX SERIES
SCHOOL OF NECESSARY MAGIC
SCHOOL OF NECESSARY MAGIC: RAINE CAMPBELL
ALISON BROWNSTONE
FEDERAL AGENTS OF MAGIC
SCIONS OF MAGIC
THE UNBELIEVABLE MR. BROWNSTONE
DWARF BOUNTY HUNTER
ACADEMY OF NECESSARY MAGIC
MAGIC CITY CHRONICLES
ROGUE AGENTS OF MAGIC
CHRONICLES OF WINLAND UNDERWOOD
WITCH WARRIOR

OTHER BOOKS BY JUDITH BERENS

OTHER BOOKS BY MARTHA CARR

JOIN THE ORICERAN UNIVERSE FAN GROUP ON FACEBOOK!

BOOKS BY MICHAEL ANDERLE

Sign up for the LMBPN email list to be notified of new releases and special deals!

http://lmbpn.com/email/

For a complete list of books by Michael Anderle, please visit:

www.lmbpn.com/ma-books/

CONNECT WITH THE AUTHORS

Martha Carr Social
Website:
http://www.marthacarr.com
Facebook:
https://www.facebook.com/groups/MarthaCarrFans/

Michael Anderle

Website: http://lmbpn.com

Email List: http://lmbpn.com/email/

https://www.facebook.com/LMBPNPublishing

https://twitter.com/MichaelAnderle

https://www.instagram.com/lmbpn_publishing/

https://www.bookbub.com/authors/michael-anderle

www.ingramcontent.com/pod-product-compliance
Lightning Source LLC
LaVergne TN
LVHW091720070526
838199LV00050B/2482